CLAIMING CHARITY

MILITARY ROMANCE — WITH A SCIENCE FICTION EDGE

ANN GIMPEL

Edited by

JENNIFER HASSANI

Illustrated by

FIONA JAYDE

CONTENTS

CLAIMING CHARITY

GENTECH REBELLION, BOOK THREE

Military Romance
(with a science fiction edge)
By
Ann Gimpel

COPYRIGHT PAGE

Book Description:

Charity's luck never ran strong because her original configuration was unstable. Her handlers designed experiments to fix the problem, but only made it worse. Sick to death of living under their thumb, she jumps at a chance to escape. She's barely settled in as a CIA special operative—a role where she can put her augmented mind and body to use—when her wobbly genetics decompensate.

Tony's a freak—a genetically altered superhuman waging war against the government. He snaps up an offer of amnesty, walking away from his role as a genetic researcher to work for the CIA. When Charity collapses in a severe seizure, he labors to save her life, but nothing's working. In a last ditch effort, he joins his mind to hers and discovers he wants her more than he's ever wanted anything. Only problem is she hates every single male freak for how they treated women in the compounds.

Charity recovers from her medical crisis, but all she can think about is Tony. Furious, determined to never let anyone like him near her, she blocks him from her mind, but he seeps back in anyway. Loving someone like Tony is a huge risk, a gamble that could throw her already volatile genes into a tailspin.

Knowing all that, why the hell is she considering it?

Series Backstory:

Sometime between the interminable wars in the Middle East and 9/11, the United States moved forward breeding a race of super humans. Clandestine labs formed, armed with eager scientists who'd always yearned to manipulate human DNA. At first the clones looked promising, growing to fighting size in as little as a dozen years, but V1 had design flaws.

Seven years ago, a rogue group turned on their creators, blew up the lab, and hit all the other breeding farms, freeing whomever they could find. In the intervening time, they've retreated to hidden compounds and created a society run by men. Women are kept on a tight leash because the men fear if they discover their innate power, they'd launch their own rebellion.

Who doesn't love a good story about a Clone War? While author Ann Gimpel's new war is happening on Earth and not on Geonosis, is it no less interesting as some real world events are pulled into the story, making it scarily plausible. What follows is an intense story that has elements of romance, adventure, intrigue and mystery. A really enjoyable read that sets up what I hope will be a pretty awesome series. TrishFLReader – Amazon Top 1000 reviewer

I absolutely loved the blend of science fiction and romance; I did not really expect that! I feel like a lot of books nowadays has only one note, especially when it comes to the science fiction genre. I haven't read a book that has successfully incorporated both elements in a while, so I was really excited to read this book. I was hooked immediately. CC2015 – Amazon Top 1000 Reviewer

Reader praise for Honor Bound, GenTech Rebellion, Book Two:
    The amazing journey continues diving into more characters and of course more frustration. Only 4 chapters in and I am enthralled. Honor is coming into her own and it is breathtaking. – Cupcakes and Books, Book Blogger

Fantastic adventure so full of action I could not put the book down until the end. Wow can you write. – Reader Review

This second book in the Gentech Rebellion Series is as action packed as the first! A fun and fast read that you will be sure to enjoy. A great mix of romance, action, and scifi-ish military. I can't wait for the third installment – Reader Review

Omg! I thought Winning Glory stopped heart! Here you get the background on Milton and Honor, two people who at first glance wouldn't mesh but click in the most profound way once you get into it. You won't regret this pick up. Start the series and hold on the edge of your seat! – Reader Review

Charity trudged across Langley's campus, the bare trees a reminder winter had months to go. Night was falling, and a chill damp seeped into her bones, exacerbated by the darkness. It had been damp in the Pacific Northwest where she lived before this, but Virginia was a close second.

Hope kept pace with her, seemingly not in a hurry. "You feeling okay?" She kept her gaze straight ahead and her tone casual, but Charity wasn't fooled.

She ground to a halt as irritation flared. "Why does everybody keep asking me that?" She tried for a moderate tone but sounded like a shrew.

Hope stopped walking too and turned to face her friend. "Because we're genetically modified—in case you've forgotten. Your genome's unstable because the bastards back at the compound where we lived tried to turn your circuitry from V3 to V4."

"Your point?" Charity gritted out.

Hope trained troubled green eyes on Charity's matching pair. "We were all worried about you. You nearly died."

"You think I'm likely to forget?" Charity punched the air. "Even if I wanted a little distance from something that scared the living shit out of me, none of you will let me ignore the slightest detail. Worse, you hammer me with it until I'd like to ram my fist down your throat to shut you up."

Hope's forehead creased into concerned lines. "Aw, hon—"

Charity made a chopping motion with one hand. "Enough. I'm fine. At least I think I am. That hideous pressure inside me before I collapsed isn't there anymore." She sucked in air, seeking a place beyond anger. "We're both tired. That last mission was a bitch."

"We need to let Faith know we're back." Hope started walking toward the building that housed their apartments.

After a pause, Charity caught up with her. "Yeah, she probably worried about us while we were gone. Her legs should be healed up by now, so she'll want to be at the meeting tomorrow at zero seven hundred."

"How'd you find out about it?" Hope angled to face her, but kept moving forward. "No one told me. I figured we'd hold off on anything for a couple days—until Milton and Honor get back from that ranch of his in Montana."

The corners of Charity's mouth twitched into half a grin. "Did you see the looks on their faces before they got out of the plane in Missoula?"

Hope snorted. "Did I ever. Milton looked like a major alpha out of a romance novel when he came out of the cockpit to scoop her up. Bet the second they got out of our sight, he backed her up against a building, ripped her pants off, and screwed her senseless."

"It probably wasn't quite that public, but I hope they're as happy as Roy and Glory," Charity murmured. "After what we lived through, we all deserve hot dudes who worship the ground we walk on."

"No kidding, huh?" Hope tipped her head to engage the retinal scanner outside their building. After a moment, the door clicked open. She nodded at the ever-present lobby guard and motioned Charity toward the stairwell. "How'd you find out about the meeting?" she persisted. "You never did tell me."

Heat traveled from her chest upward, and Charity chided herself for a much-too-human reaction to Tony, one of the genetically altered men who'd defected to help the CIA. "From Tony. Guess Charlie told him to pass it down the line."

"Sheesh. Charlie's our team leader. You'd think he could tell us himself."

"He and Roy were called into a meeting with the brass. I suppose they got tapped because Milton isn't here." Charity trotted into the stairwell behind Hope. None of them liked elevators. They'd come from a life where they trained six to eight hours a day. By contrast, life at the CIA compound was soft and cushy.

When Charity walked through the door at the top of the stairwell, Faith raced toward them, a huge grin on her face. Before Charity could say a word, Faith hugged them both soundly murmuring, "I'm damned glad you're back. When I felt your energy, I couldn't just wait in my apartment. Had to lay eyes on you."

"Oh ye of little faith." Charity made a pun. "Did you think we were so feeble we couldn't get through a raid on the Nameless Ones' headquarters?"

Faith let go, so excited she bounced up and down. Like all of them, she was six feet tall, with waist-length black hair and cat green eyes. Today, she wore gray sweats emblazoned with the CIA logo. "Tell me what happened. Everything. I was afraid you'd skip bothering me until morning, and by then curiosity would've swallowed me whole." She swept an appraising glance over them. "You probably want to clean up. I'll tag along, and you can fill me in."

"Good plan." Charity nodded, so tired her bones mimicked lead pipes attached to her muscles with baling wire that poked every time she moved. "Feel free to link up with me, and then Hope can join us after her shower."

Faith pushed the stairwell door open and stared down it before turning to face the other women. Her smile faded, replaced by a pinched look. "Where's Honor? I know Glory's with Roy, but—"

"In Montana with Milton at a cattle ranch." Hope waggled her eyebrows suggestively.

Faith exhaled briskly and broke into laughter. "Awesome! I wish them every happiness. Come on. Let's get moving, so you can tell me everything. I want all the dirty details."

Charity covered the fifty feet to her door and tilted her chin so the retinal scanner would let her into her apartment. Faith stuck to her like a shadow.

"See you soon." Hope's voice echoed as she moved farther down the hall to her quarters.

"How are the legs?" Charity asked and sat to unlace her muddy boots, which she then toed off, followed by her socks.

"Healed. I'm back at a hundred percent." Faith beamed. "I was good to go about twenty-four hours after you left, but by then it was too late." She made a face. "Like the CIA would've sent a special plane with just me in it. What the hell happened? It was like a funeral home around here for those few hours when everyone was certain Milton was dead."

"Wasn't real cheery where we were, either." Charity stood and unzipped her field jacket, hanging it on a hook. She systematically stripped off the rest of her clothes as she walked into her bedroom. Flipping the laundry hamper open, she chucked everything inside.

"What exactly happened?" Faith persisted. I never did find out."

"Basically, the Nameless Ones booby-trapped the underground escape passageway leading to the subterranean computer room. Milton made it to the room before the explosion, but he couldn't let any of us know because the chamber's shielded with metal. Follow me if you want to hear more."

Charity trudged into the small bathroom. Feeling stretched thin, she turned on the shower and got under its spray. So she wouldn't have to shout, she switched to telepathy, realizing as she did so that Faith could've stayed put. *Anyway, I guess Milton tried to merge with the computer—like we do—decided he didn't know enough to go that route, and so he stole the hard drives instead.*

"How'd he get out if the tunnels were blown to bits?"

"I'm a little hazy on that, but I guess there was another passageway he discovered by accident."

"Thank God for that. We need him."

Charity thought about that as she sluiced shampoo from her hair. She'd lived in a dorm with eleven other women at a special hidden compound for seven years. Hundreds of similar compounds were located throughout the world. Her memory of her life before the compound was nonexistent, as if someone erased that part of her central processing unit. She turned off the water before drawing the curtain aside.

Faith handed her a towel. "You're pretty quiet."

"I was thinking about what you said. The part about needing Milton." She blotted water from her body and then grabbed a dry towel to wind around her head. "I understand he's the head of the CIA and singlehandedly responsible for deciding we were worth rescuing, but for years the only ones we needed were us."

"When it got down to it…" Faith shot a pointed glance her way. "Seven of us didn't trust Glory enough to go with her the night she offered us a chance at freedom."

Charity winced. Those seven women were dead, a point that still made her heart hurt. The twelve of them had been like sisters, united against the men—Nameless Ones—and their ironclad control over all the women. Even simple things like food, heat, and clothing were rationed.

The genetically altered men rode herd on them because the women's design was so far superior, but she hadn't known it then. Even if she had, it wouldn't have mattered. No excuse in the universe was good enough to justify how they'd been treated. The Nameless Ones' strict rules rankled, until the women wanted nothing more than to wipe out every last one of them.

Glory had killed one of the men—to sidestep being raped. It was why she ran away: to avoid living out the rest of her life in an iso cell. But if she hadn't run, she'd never have met Roy, and Charity and the others would still be stuck in their compound, functioning as one step up from slaves.

Charity made her way past Faith. She rustled clean navy blue sweats from a drawer and pulled them on over her still-damp body. A sharp tap at the door announced Hope on the other side. Charity sent a mental blast of energy to twist the locking mechanism.

"Hiya!" Hope's hair hung down her back in damp curls. She hugged Faith. "All caught up, hon?"

"Pretty much. Any idea what comes next?"

"Not really. Are either of you hungry?"

"Me!" Charity snugged her feet into a pair of running shoes.

"I'll keep you company if you're headed for the cafeteria." Faith patted her hips. "Probably don't need another meal, but I can have a cup of coffee."

Charity glanced at her. "You don't look heavier."

"I'm probably not, but I couldn't get much exercise while my broken legs healed, and the only thing left to do was eat." She shrugged. "Let's get some food into the two of you. Bet you'd love to have an uninterrupted night's sleep."

"Last night wasn't so bad," Charity cut in. "We were in the Air Force barracks in Colorado Springs. At least Hope and I were. Glory was with Roy, and Honor was with Milton."

"Yeah, you already mentioned that." Faith smirked. "Sounds like someone's wishing for a guy all for herself."

An image of Tony—tall, muscled, gorgeous with his shaggy dark hair and penetrating eyes—blasted out of some underground reservoir to taunt her. It felt so real, Charity's breath hitched.

"Shut up." She mock slugged Faith before grabbing a coat and leading the way out of her apartment. She'd spent the last seven years hating Nameless Ones. Hell would freeze over before she paid the slightest heed to Tony's attentiveness. He probably just wanted to get laid, but she was less than interested.

Yeah. Just keep telling myself that. Maybe if I hear it enough, I'll believe it.

He saved my life, a different inner voice cut in.
So what? It doesn't mean I owe him shit.

TONY DIALED his night vision up another notch and paced Frank as they ran hard around Langley's perimeter. After being cooped up for hours in a plane, both men needed to burn off some steam. As Tony ran, scenes from his computer-like brain flashed before him.

After his petri dish birth on one of the breeding farms set up by the U.S. government, he'd been groomed from adolescence to work as a genetic researcher. None of them attended school; their knowledge was downloaded directly from huge mainframes operated by government scientists. He lived a comfortable life at his breeding farm near Portland, Oregon, but it blew up in his face seven years ago. He was twenty-two then and knee-deep in research to perfect those like him. Each successive strain was a bit better than the last, but problems still cropped up.

He'd been close to a major breakthrough—at least he thought he was, but it could've been a dead end like so much of his research—when a cadre of renegade freaks, genetically engineered humans just like him, staged a rebellion. They hadn't cared for the decision to scrap the earlier prototypes, so they blew up every breeding farm they could find. After that, they created hidden compounds, like the one in Keyser, West Virginia where Tony ended up.

He hadn't bought into the violence, but there wasn't a hell of a lot of choice once it began. Normal humans shot them on sight after the rebellion, so he went along with the program and resurrected his genetic research projects at his assigned compound. He didn't have nearly the access to materials he had prior to the rebellion, but at least he was still alive.

"You're pretty quiet, buddy," Frank observed.

"Sorry. I was thinking."

The other man snorted. "Always dangerous. About what? Did

you come up with something we missed on those hard drives Milton swiped from our headquarters?"

"Nah. Wish it were that straightforward."

Frank slugged him in the arm. "Watch that esoteric stuff. Our programming's not designed for it."

"Maybe not, but do you ever wonder what will become of us?"

"The probability of that line of thought producing something of value is—"

"Not what I asked," Tony snapped. "We've thrown in our lot with normal humans, V0 as it were. We can't undo it."

"So? You and I discussed this before we showed ourselves and requested amnesty. We could've remained hidden. They would have found Charity without our help, and then they'd have left. We didn't take that route. Are you having second thoughts?"

"Not really. We didn't fit in with the other Nameless Ones—a ridiculous moniker since we had names, we just didn't tell them to the women." Tony slowed when they came to a perimeter fence and turned to face the other man. Because of the physical strength built into his genetics, he wasn't even slightly winded.

Frank stopped and tossed his hood back. Unkempt black hair fell to his shoulders, and he examined Tony through amber, animal-like eyes with vertical slit pupils. All the men looked very much the same due to shared genetics. Tall, rangy, muscled. Both of them wore regulation issue CIA field gear they hadn't changed out of yet.

"What aren't you saying?" Frank asked.

"Not sure. Except I'm feeling like a man without a country. We didn't fit in there, but we don't fit in here, either. They don't trust us. I saw it in Milton's eyes that night you and I saved Charity's life."

Frank grimaced. "Shit, bro. We're machines. We're not supposed to have feelings. Who cares if they trust us, so long as they continue to offer us a place to work and live? When did you fall off the wagon?"

Should I?

Tony weighed the advisability of confiding in Frank, but if not him, whom?

"Talk, or I'm going back to my apartment. I'm fine when we're moving, but I'm getting cold. Can't be much more than fifteen degrees out here. In fact," Frank sent a short blurt of power outward, "it's eighteen point three Fahrenheit, but there's a five knot wind, which brings the ambient temperature to—"

"Never mind that. I know it's cold without a weather report. I have a problem that runs deeper than the humans not trusting us. They made a commitment to us, same as we did to them. The odds of them welching on the deal—so long as we don't fuck them over—is under twelve percent."

Frank furled his brows. "Okay. So you have a problem. Is it something we could hash out inside where it's warm?"

"I think better when I'm cold."

"Fine." Frank gestured with a gloved hand. "Whatever it is, get it out, so we can chase down something to eat and find our beds."

Tony unclenched his jaw. It was either spit it out or shut up. Running probabilities about Frank's reaction wouldn't alter his choices. He squared his shoulders and began to talk. "I spent a long time—hours—linked to Charity when she was so compromised. I was the one who sent my energy into her."

"I haven't forgotten. So?"

"I developed a fondness for her during that time." Very unmachine-like feelings tightened Tony's gut.

Frank's eyes widened. "Oh ho! You want to fuck her. I'm not seeing where that's a problem. The women were off limits to us at the compounds, but the CIA doesn't have those kind of rules."

The unmachine-like feelings intensified, and Tony felt his face grow warm. "Yeah, I want her that way, but it's more than that. I like her. She's a bitch, sure, but she's fresh and funny and spunky. We drummed the spirit out of so many of the women, but not her."

"Have you talked with her about any of this?"

Tony shook his head. "No."

"Why not? Seems to me that'd be the logical place to start."

A snort blew past Tony's lips. "Yeah, huh? Problem is I got a pretty good look inside her head. She hates us."

Frank drew back. "Why? She never even met us before she and her group attacked our compound."

Tony shook his head again. "It runs deeper than that. She hates all of us men—for how we treated her and the other women. Even if that weren't there, it must've been appalling for her when she discovered the V4s slaughtered the females in our compound. Her team planned to rescue them. The V4s figured it out and beat them to the punch."

"Yeah, but none of that was personal—" Frank began.

"Try telling her that. I'm sure it felt goddamned personal. Christ! The women's bodies weren't even cold when Charity stumbled onto them."

"I'm not sure Charity found them, but the women who did certainly told her about it." Frank jerked his chin in the general direction of their apartment building. "Let's get moving." When Tony fell into step with him, he went on. "Seems to me you've really only got two choices. One. You suck it up and keep quiet. We weren't exactly designed to have mates. All our babies were created in test tubes—even after the breeding farms."

"That was because we were afraid the women would pick our brains during sex, discover how powerful they were, and demand equality."

"It doesn't matter why," Frank replied. "Even though I was a minority, I never believed it would've been the end of the world if the women discovered their innate power, but they didn't. Regardless, over time, we got away from intercourse as a primary source of procreation."

"We're getting off course. What's my second option?"

"Sit down and talk to her. Tell her how you feel."

Tony had considered that before, and he rolled the probabilities of how such a conversation might go through his brain. "Less than an eighteen percent chance she'd be open to it," he muttered.

Frank didn't respond, and they ran the rest of the way to their building in silence. Once they were inside, Tony said, "Thanks."

"For what? I didn't help much. See you tomorrow at zero seven hundred." Frank turned down the hallway that led to his apartment.

Tony climbed a flight of stairs to his quarters and let himself in. If getting something going with Charity was such a crapshoot, why couldn't he let go of the idea?

When the answer came, he didn't like it much. He'd broken protocol to save her, blending his energy with hers in an intimate pattern that wasn't in any of the manuals. Apparently she'd gotten under his skin during the process, and now he was stuck. When he wasn't busy, she was all he thought about.

He stripped out of his heavy field coat and tossed it over a chair. The rest of his clothes ended up in a heap on the floor. Everything could stand a tour through the washing machine, but not tonight. He headed for the bathroom and a shower with his cock standing out like a ship's prow. He was hard almost all the time now, despite jacking off two or three times a day. Hard because he wanted her.

Crap!

He pulled the shower curtain aside. Once he got the water going, he stepped over the high rim of the tub. Even though he tried not to, his hands found their way to his engorged flesh, and somewhere between the soap and hot water, he made himself come with visions of what he thought Charity's perfect, naked body would look like plastered behind his eyes.

CHAPTER 2

Charity slept like a dead thing. Even though she instructed her brain to exit sleep mode, she felt fuzzy. Two cups of instant coffee later, her mind still wasn't quite as sharp as she liked. Figuring more coffee wouldn't help, she trotted smartly down the stairs. Once she got to the door, she pulled her coat closer to her body against the chill morning before letting herself outside. Stuffing her hands into her pockets, she jogged toward the meeting room a few buildings over. It was near Milton's office, and when she thought about him, she realized how much she'd miss Honor. Not that she begrudged her friend time with the man she was obviously falling in love with, but still, the women had formed a tight unit for so long, the idea of a man siphoning off any of the good mojo was disconcerting. Try as she might, she couldn't hate Milton, though. He and Roy, Glory's almost husband, were deucedly decent men.

She blew out a breath and watched it plume in the frosty air, surprised she'd slept as well as she had. Her ambivalence about Tony was so disturbing, she knew she'd have to do something. Scrubbing him from her memory circuits wasn't an option since she had to work with him every day. About the time she reached the building, an idea formed. He was like any other man, right? That meant, if she started flirting outrageously with someone else, maybe he'd get disgusted and stop sending those warm looks her way. The ones that made her feel like she was melting from the inside out.

Nice try.

What does flirting look like?

How would I even go about it?

She trudged up the stairs, running scenarios from movies and television shows that featured boy-meets-girl plot lines. By the time she got to the conference room, she was smiling. It wasn't all that hard. All you had to do was throw your body around, and men came running. A come hither look or two, and they were malleable as watered down clay.

"You're looking refreshed this morning." Tony walked over to her with a big smile on his face. "Can I get you a cup of coffee?"

An uncomfortable, fluttery sensation jabbed her midsection, and Charity pivoted away so he couldn't see her face. When she felt him probing the edges of her mind, she slapped up a barrier and turned back to face him, squaring her shoulders. "Actually, I feel like crap. And I already had my coffee."

A worried look crossed his face, adding small lines around his eyes. "Do you need Frank and me to do another check of your circuitry?"

Charity sucked in a sharp breath. That was damn near the last thing she wanted. She was vulnerable when they mucked around inside her head. He might see her confused welter of feelings about him. "No. I'm not having those kind of problems again."

"Then what's wrong?" He persisted, but the question was kind, not pointed.

"Nothing. Nothing's wrong. I'm going to sit down." She made her way to the women's side of the table, forcing her gaze straight ahead. She wanted to look back at him, but it'd be the wrong thing to do. In its own way, his obvious caring was harder to deal with than the men's overbearing attitudes had been back at the compound. At least she could erect blockades to keep arrogance and authoritarian mindsets at bay. Turning away from kindness was much harder.

The five men on Roy's team filed in, mostly with coffee cups in hand. Like Roy, they were tall, rangy, and bulging with muscle. No matter what color hair they'd been born with, all of them wore their hair black now. It blended better with the night, made them less obvious when they pitted themselves against danger.

David, the one she knew best after Charlie, nodded at her before he sat down and laced his fingers together in front of him.

Faith walked through the door. She poured herself a cup of coffee and made her way to the seat next to Charity. "Morning, hon. Sleep okay?"

"We're machines. We always *sleep okay*. It's just a matter of—"

Faith sent her such a hurt look, Charity couldn't continue. Because she didn't know quite what to say, she focused on Charlie and Roy, standing at the front of the room. Both men looked grim, and she wondered what new catastrophe landed in their laps during the night.

Hope took a seat on her other side and muttered, "Incoming."

"Yeah," Charity said. "I was just thinking the same thing."

Faith leaned toward them. "Do you two know something I don't?"

"No," Charity replied, "but just look at them." She angled her glance toward the front of the room.

"Seats, everyone," Roy barked. "Now. We're five minutes late as it is."

"Uncle Miltie would've already started the meeting," Charlie observed, *sotto voce*.

"Yeah, well, he's a bigger hard ass than me." Roy glanced around the room with his shrewd blue eyes. Around six feet two, his coppery hair was dyed black like all the men on his special ops team. He was lean, mean, all hard muscles and no nonsense, but whenever he looked at Glory, the harsh planes of his face softened like they were right now.

Even without the obvious cue from Roy, Charity sensed Glory's energy as she ran into the room and slid into a seat. "Sorry I'm late." Color spread across her cheeks, and Charity could guess why she wasn't quite on time. Roy probably would've been late too, except apparently he could get dressed faster. Or maybe he'd just unzipped himself for a morning quickie…

Heat rose to Charity's face, and she redirected her thoughts. *Shit. Fuck. Damn.* All roads led to sex. She had a big problem. Clearly, she needed a man. Anyone with a dick would do right about now.

"Charity!" Charlie's voice was sharp.

Her head snapped up, and she realized she'd been studying the tabletop intently. "Sir?"

"Nice to have your attention."

"Sorry, mister team leader. Sir."

"Enough of that," Roy cut in. "We need to get down to it. There were more attacks last night. They hit the CDC again and NYC Medical Center."

"Why didn't you wake us?" Faith asked.

"Protocol," Charlie shot a gimlet glance her way, "is to wait until your team leaders are done talking and solicit questions from you."

Faith rolled her eyes. "Look. We weren't raised in your world. I asked a good question."

"You'll get an answer," Charlie said. "Keep listening."

Even though she didn't mean to, Charity glanced sidelong at Tony. His dark brows were drawn into a thick, worried line. When she probed, she found a phalanx of questions in his mind.

"Keep going, then," Frank urged gruffly, aiming his comment at Charlie.

"Yeah," Tony broke in. "So we can get to the Q and A part."

Roy and Charlie exchanged a pointed glance. Roy nodded sharply and Charlie said, "I've been monitoring this situation since zero three thirty. For once, no one was hurt, but the freaks—" He frowned. "Sorry, folks, but it's so much easier than saying genetically altered humans every single time. Anyway, it appears they were after a very specific drug. They wiped out the entire supply in both places."

Frank pounded his fist on the table. "Screw protocol. They took Cortexiphan, didn't they?"

"Huh?" Charity stared at him after a quick search of her memory banks. "That's a made up drug from that TV show. The weird one. *Fringe.*"

"It's not made up," Faith mumbled.

Tony settled his gaze on Charity and repeated what Faith said. "It's not made up. Somehow, the writers for that show found out about the drug. The breeding farms were still operative then, and several scientists pitched a fit about them outing Cortexiphan."

"I remember that." Roy spoke slowly. "I was quite a few years out of law school and working here. It was a big fat fucking mess—I even wrote up a legal opinion on it—but freedom of the press prevailed. The drug never made it past experimental status, and its name wasn't patented, so no one could do shit when the television show swiped the name."

"Besides, the argument was no one would believe it was real," Frank said.

"It worked," David chimed in. "People assumed it was just another off-the-wall aspect of a woo-woo television series."

'Yeah. If I'm remembering right, it was so beyond the pale, the series didn't run very many seasons," another of Roy's team added.

Charity tried to keep her mouth shut and wait until Charlie asked for questions, but everybody else was taking, so she dove in. "I don't care about a defunct TV show. What exactly does the drug do in the real world?"

"Two things." Tony spoke up. "It can even out people with your unstable genome problems, and it maximizes psi potential for everyone—human and our kin alike."

"If that's true," Glory said, "why isn't it in general use?"

"It has a hell of a side effect punch," Frank replied. "Worse for humans, though. Much worse. Statistically, forty-three point six percent of those who are dosed with it develop a significant delusional disorder. One that's not amenable to treatment with psychiatric drugs. Eight percent die, and an additional seventeen percent become so paranoid they're worthless."

"What are the percentages for us?" Faith asked.

"It varies," Frank replied. "Anywhere from less than three percent to seven." He paused, narrowing his eyes in thought. "While those might not appear insignificant, our side effects aren't nearly as debilitating as those experienced by humans."

Tony twisted to face Roy and Charlie. "How much did they steal?"

"According to the keepers of the keys at both institutions," Roy said, "enough to dose several thousand people. Basically, they filched something like ninety-eight percent of the total stores nationwide. There's another small cache in south Florida that I assume they decided was too small to bother with."

"Crap!" Tony shook his head. "We've got to figure out where they took it and get it back."

A harsh smile, totally lacking in humor, stretched across Roy's face. "No shit. You just outlined our mission to a tee. We're going to track the Cortexiphan and do whatever's required to recover it."

"There's no choice," Frank said. "Not really. Our erstwhile brethren stole enough of the drug to fix their genome problems, turn everyone into a functional version of V4, and make themselves invincible. We have a little time, but not much. They need to titrate the chemical through a series of specialized filters to strengthen its potential."

"We used to dream about getting hold of Cortexiphan," Tony added. "Never could figure out a way to get it out of its hidey holes without calling undue attention to ourselves. It was impossible to synthesize without securing materials that would've exposed us." He paused. "At that point in the game, our marching orders were to maintain virtual invisibility. We'd go after things we needed, but only if we thought we could get in and out without being noticed.

Stealing the raw materials to synthesize the drug would've been a dead giveaway, since no one but us would want to make more of it."

"Obviously, whoever's running the show is getting desperate," Frank said. "Breaking into the CDC was bold. That medical center was likely easier. Why'd they have Cortexiphan, anyway?"

"Because no one would think to look there," Charlie said sourly. "In addition to our other problems, I'm guessing freaks infiltrated the CDC. It would explain how they were able to pull off the heist in the first place. And how they knew about NYC Medical."

"I understand why we need to get it back, but what happens if we fail?" Charity kept a tremor out of her voice. The one thing she feared most was being forced back into a compound. Death would be preferable.

"We won't fail." Charlie's piercing expression matched Roy's. "One thing in our favor is the freaks were in a hurry, so they took the drug in locked metal canisters, which have tracking devices."

Tony shook his head. "They'll remove them."

"They already did," Roy concurred, "but not before they traveled quite a way from Atlanta and New York City. The devices were embedded in the canister material, which meant the freaks had to work their way past the locks and remove the sealed glass drug tubes from their packing materials." He stopped to take a breath. "It narrows our search parameters considerably. At least I hope it does." Moving to the front of the room, he flipped switches until a wall map of the United States blinked into being with lights denoting each compound.

"They removed one set of tracking devices here." He pointed to Bangor, Maine. "And the other set here." He tapped New Orleans, Louisiana. "Our first guess is they didn't want to risk examining the canisters until they put some distance between themselves and the sites they hit. Plus, we determined they left by private jet. Not much chance of jettisoning a tracking device from thirty thousand feet."

"We believe," Charlie cut in, "if we narrow our search to the half dozen compounds nearest to where we located the tracking devices, we have a good chance of finding the drug."

Glory glanced at Frank and Tony. "Thoughts?"

Frank made a rude sound. "Lots of them, none particularly good."

Tony got to his feet and made his way to Roy's side in front of the map. He peered at it, his face screwed into a scowl. "If I had to guess," he said after a lengthy silence, "they took the drugs here and here." He pointed to a compound north of New Orleans and a second one south of Bangor, fronting the North Atlantic. "They're where our primary research lab sites are. If the freaks were going to prepare large amounts of the drug for our people, those are the logical places."

Roy nodded sharply. "I need to confer with my bosses. My first inclination is to simply bomb the fuck out of both sites, but the brass may not agree." He glanced at the clock. "Meet back here in two hours. In the meantime, hit the practice arena and work on that mind meld stuff. If I get vetoed, we'll need to move on one of those sites. There aren't enough of us to split forces."

"What about those extra teams that were supposed to train with us?" Glory asked.

"They're *en route*, but there's not time to get them up to speed before we have to move out," Charlie answered.

Charity chewed her lower lip. It seemed to her that having more firepower, even from freak-naïve troops would be better than going in light, but she didn't say anything.

"You have your orders, folks," Roy said. "Back here at eleven hundred. Make sure you've eaten in case we deploy right after that."

"One more thing," Frank spoke up.

Roy nodded sharply. "What? Be quick about it."

"We've never used any sort of air transport. If the freaks used jet aircraft, they had to be either chartered—or stolen. Most likely the latter."

Roy pulled a long face. "That's right. The lot of you can figure out how to fly them by linking to their onboard computers." He thinned his lips into a terse line. "Regardless if they were stolen or hired, there'll be a record somewhere, and we can maybe get a visual on who we're hunting. I'll get our surveillance techs working on it."

Chairs scraped as people got to their feet. Glory made a beeline for Roy, and the two of them put their heads together. Hope and Faith flanked Charity. "What do you think?" Hope asked as they walked out the door.

"I don't know what to think," Charity replied. "The Nameless Ones sure as fuck upped the ante."

"Do either of you know anything about this Cortexiphan?" Hope asked as they made their way down the stairs and outside.

"I know a little," Faith said. "I used to work with the geneticists, and I remember them drooling over the possibilities in that substance."

"Did they ever try to synthesize it?" Charity asked.

"Oh sure. Lots of times, but we didn't have the sophisticated machinery we needed. Or the chemicals." Faith rolled her eyes. "Whoever planned the rebellion had shit for brains. There were so many things at the breeding farms we could've used, but they blew sky high, right along with the farms."

"Interesting," Charity muttered.

Frank and Tony caught up with them when they were halfway to the building that held the underground practice arena. "Ladies." Frank inclined his head. Something about his expression broadcast enthusiasm, blended with a healthy dose of curiosity.

"You look like you can't wait to get your teeth into this problem," Hope observed.

He nodded, looking thoughtful. "It's one fascinating son of a bitch. There were times I'd have killed to get my hands on Cortexiphan. For example, if we'd had some here, we could have injected Charity with it at the first sign of instability, and the problem would've fixed itself."

Breath whooshed from Charity's lungs. "Really? It's that powerful?"

Frank nodded. "And then some. Most of the problems humans experience with it don't happen to us."

"Yes, it's definitely a win-win." Tony was silent for a beat. "Actually, it'd be great to keep some here. If there are going to be more of us, that is."

"Maybe if we approach those compounds from the ground, rather than blowing them up…" Charity swallowed the rest of her words. She'd love it if more of her kin left the dark side, but it felt like too much to hope for.

"I was thinking the same thing," Faith said. "Sorry for eavesdropping on your thoughts, but I'd like more of us here too. I can envision the CIA doing an aerial raid on the Maine compound. It's in open country, and the collateral damage would be manageable, but the one in Louisiana is in a long-settled area."

"How have we kept it secret?" Charity asked.

"It's hidden in an alligator-infested swamp," Tony said. "But Faith is correct, there are farms and antebellum mansions nearby."

Roy's team ran around them with a collection of high-five signs. Charlie and Glory were with them, hooting and whistling as they passed by.

"Hey!" Faith shouted. "They're going to beat us to the arena."

"Not!" Hope took off at a dead run with Faith on her heels.

Charity started after them, but Tony closed his hand around her arm. "Stay here for a moment. Talk with me."

It was tempting. So tempting. And such a bad idea, she refused to even consider it. At the bottom of everything, he was still a Nameless One. Never mind, he'd switched sides and worked for the CIA now.

"I don't fucking think so." She wrenched out of his grip and raced after the other women.

CHAPTER 3

Tony watched the bounce of Charity's backside as she ran away from him. Had he said something wrong? Was his request to remain so they could talk too pointed? Maybe she was frightened he'd push the issue of examining the stability of her circuits.

"Come on." Frank's voice held a gruff edge. "Looks like you got your answer."

"What answer?" Tony followed Frank into the building, and they jogged to the bank of elevators. The practice arena was a hundred feet underground. If there were stairs leading to it, he'd never located them.

"That dilemma you outlined last night. I'm guessing you chose door number two, but it's apparent she doesn't want to talk." Frank brushed his palms together and ducked into the elevator. "Makes it easy. Case closed."

Tony joined him and watched the stainless steel doors slide shut. The case may be closed, but it didn't feel easy—or straightforward. Besides he didn't want it to be closed. She had to talk with him, goddammit. His request hadn't been unreasonable.

Frank swung Tony to face him. "I'm only going to say this once.

23

The Cortexiphan heist is critical. I need all your brainpower focused on it. Not on Charity. She's not a good bet anyway."

"Why would you say that?"

"Because she's not stable. You may have salvaged her, but who knows how long the fix will last."

Tony felt oddly defensive. "It could be permanent."

"It could be, but often it's not. Anyway, your love life's not our priority. If you just want to get laid, pick one of the clerical pool. I've seen them making eyes at us."

Tony snapped his mouth shut. It wasn't worth mentioning that he didn't only want sex. Frank wouldn't understand. Tony had worked with the other genetically modified human for several years —plenty long enough to appreciate how he ticked.

The doors swooshed open, and Tony marched through, leading the way down a long hallway lined with lockers and into a state-of-the-art practice arena. It even had something like a holodeck straight out of *Star Trek*. Men's and women's shower areas were at opposite ends of the gym, along with bunks for the times when they trained two and three days straight and needed a few hours of sleep.

"Over here." Charlie motioned them to the far end of the gym where he was pairing a member from Roy's team with each of the women. "Tony, you and David will work together. Frank, you'll partner with me."

The rest of Charlie's instructions soaked into Tony's computer-like brain, but he wasn't truly listening. He was focused on Charity and the man she'd drawn to work with. Like all of Roy's team, Chris was one lean, mean dude with close-cropped black hair. His hazel gaze was fixed intently on Charity, and Tony wanted to land his fist right between his eyes, tell Chris she was off limits—

Frank poked Tony hard in the side, bringing his thoughts to an abrupt halt. Shaking his head sharply, Frank shot a stern glance Tony's way before he followed Charlie to where they'd work on melding their minds to immobilize large numbers of freaks for long enough to storm their fortresses. Frank didn't need to say anything, or employ telepathy. His meaning was clear enough: forget the woman, focus on getting the Cortexiphan back.

Tony nodded at David, and the two of them shook hands before walking briskly toward a private corner of the enormous room. Charity and Chris staked out their own corner. It might be Tony's imagination, but she was walking pretty fucking close to him. When she looked Chris' way and smiled, something dark and unpleasant slammed into Tony's gut.

"It's none of my business," David's deep voice rumbled, "but looks like you've got it bad."

Tony dragged his attention away from Charity. "Huh? I don't understand what you mean."

David furled his brows as if he didn't quite believe Tony and jerked his chin toward Charity and Chris. "The woman. You like her, but she doesn't want anything to do with you."

Tony snapped his jaws together so hard his teeth clanked against each other. Was everybody a goddamned advice maven? First Frank, now David.

"Never mind." David hurried on. "I said it was none of my business—and it's not, but one thing you might want to consider is the women had seven years to nurture ill will toward you." He swung to face Tony. "We're far enough from the others. Stop walking. To close off the other deal, from what I understand, the women were one step up from slaves—"

Anger flared, hot and unexpected; it sparred with jealousy and turned Tony's stomach into a twisted mass of pain. "Stop right there. We didn't beat the women. We didn't rape them."

David squared his shoulders. "No, but you didn't extend them any freedom, either. From what Glory told us, you punished them in isolation cells, and they never had enough to eat."

"None of us had enough to eat. We couldn't exactly hit the local markets and maintain invisibility, so we raised our food. It took years to figure out how to farm effectively..." Tony realized he was defending a way of life that was indefensible, so he shut up.

"I'm sorry." David stuck his hand out again. "Didn't mean to bring up anything painful." He rolled his eyes. "Actually, I was going to commiserate. I've had my share of female problems. This job. It's not conducive to most women's ideas of connubial bliss. They like to have us front and center, not running off with our faces blacked out at zero three hundred."

Tony smiled at the visual. "No, I suppose not. Although, I don't know all that much about human culture because I spent most of my time in the lab. The women, now they had more opportunity to watch movies and surf the Internet."

"Movies, TV, and the Net aren't the best places to learn about any culture. Ready to rumble?"

"If by that you mean am I ready to begin, the answer is yes. Open your mind to me. Maybe while we're linked, I'll discover more of your secrets about the care and feeding of women."

"Good luck with that." David broke into a laugh. "About the only luck I have is getting into their beds. I don't have much of a track record beyond that."

Tony shrugged. "I'll take it, since I don't even have that much. When you're starting with zero, you need all the help you can get."

CHARITY SMILED AT CHRIS. Maybe he'd provide an answer to at least one of her problems. She wasn't particularly attracted to him, but he did like women, and he'd be more than willing to service her. She'd seen it in his mind while they were linked. Maybe things wouldn't even have to go as far as sex. If she could flirt a little, it might get Tony to leave her alone. A small, forlorn place with unpleasantly sharp edges opened inside her. It took a little fiddling with her circuitry before she understood she didn't want Tony to leave her alone. Not really.

I can't hook up with a Nameless One. I just can't.

It'd only be a matter of time before his true colors surfaced, and then I'd be fucked. In more ways than one.

"Charity?" Chris laid a hand on her arm. "Are you all right?" His hazel eyes radiated concern.

Of course not. "Sure. Just peachy."

"Want to practice that last move again?" A smile warmed his eyes. "I think I've almost got it."

"Fantastic! Let's do it." Grateful for a retreat into work, she linked with Chris. Partway through their next series of mental maneuvers, Charlie's voice dragged her out of their mind meld.

"Roy wants all of us back in the meeting room now. It's earlier than he anticipated, so lunch will be waiting. Get moving." Charlie clapped his hands smartly together. "Go. Go. Go."

Charity heard excitement zing beneath Charlie's command and rolled her mental eyes. Men. All the ones here were adrenaline junkies, but if they didn't live to be deployed, they'd have picked different careers.

Chris paced her as they left the room and joined the small group waiting for the elevator that would move them to ground level. She glanced sidelong at Tony, only to interrupt him doing the same thing to her.

Damn!

She saw speculation in his eyes, so maybe her ploy to suck up to another man just might buy her what she needed. Once the elevator spit them out, she sprinted through the door and set a course across Langley's campus, not caring who chose to follow her. The only important thing was their next mission and making certain the Nameless Ones didn't have ammunition to turn themselves into a super race that could truly wipe out humankind. Charity wasn't under any illusions. No matter how she felt about normal humans—and she was ambivalent—they were a hundred times better than Nameless Ones.

The *raison d'être* for the breeding farms had been to create a race of indomitable soldiers. If the rebellion hadn't happened, who knew what the human scientists would've come up with? The next seven years—the ones after the rebellion—hadn't yielded much. Rumors circulated that their own scientists—men like Frank and Tony— were closing on a flawless version, except it never happened.

She slapped her palm against the scanner and moved into the building where the meeting would be, still deep in thought.

Chris panted from behind her. "Christ, lady. You run like the wind. Couldn't catch up until you slowed to open the door." He grabbed the stairwell door and held it for her.

"Thanks." She shot what she hoped was a sunny smile his way and took the stairs three at a time. Good. Let Chris hover. It might have the desired effect, and she wouldn't have to do a damned thing beyond appearing approachable.

I thought I wanted to get laid.

Yeah, but Chris doesn't feel right.

An unpleasant truth rocked her. No one felt right except Tony. Just her rotten luck, the one she wanted would spell disaster.

Roy greeted her at the door and directed her to a table in the back of the room where sandwiches sat piled on trays, along with tubs of macaroni and potato salad and a selection of soda and water. She got her lunch and made her way to a seat. The others did the same, and for a few minutes the only sounds in the room were chewing and swallowing. Tony had taken the seat directly across from her, so it was tough to totally ignore him.

"Look sharp." Roy's voice snapped her attention toward the front of the room where he stood. When she truly looked at him, she noticed he was in full field regalia. Camos, Kevlar vest, and weaponry hanging off his lean form. So they were on their way to somewhere—and pretty damned soon from the looks of things.

"Eat while you listen," Roy continued. "We're leaving at twelve hundred. Finish your lunch, return to your quarters, dress in your moderate weather field gear, and meet at the flight line. Stop by the arms master for munitions and ammo." Roy eyed Frank, Tony, and the women. "I know you don't fully appreciate weaponry, but trust me when I tell you it's essential to deal with snakes and alligators where we're going."

Charity should've learned her lesson earlier that day about keeping quiet, but words slipped out anyway. "Let me guess." She quirked a brow. "We're not going to Maine."

"Our objective is the Louisiana compound," Roy went on as if she hadn't said anything. "My men have had experience navigating through swamps. How about the rest of you?"

"We have." Frank gestured at Tony. "We spent some time at that compound, so we can help you find it. I understand you have coordinates, but that swamp is a bitch. You already mentioned snakes and alligators, but many of the waterways don't go through."

"Fucking great," David muttered. Roy shot him a look, and he shook his head. "Sorry, boss."

"A jet will fly us to Barksdale Air Force Base. From there, we'll switch to a chopper, followed by zodiac inflatable rafts, courtesy of the Joint Reserve Naval Air Base near New Orleans."

Charity pulled up the map program that lived in her head. "Isn't Barksdale at the wrong end of the state?" she asked.

Roy nodded. "It's in the extreme northwest corner, but it's the closest base and the only one in Louisiana. We'll need aerial backup on this one—in case things go to hell."

Charlie straightened in his chair. "What's the plan after we get the zodiacs, sir?"

Roy pushed buttons, and a topographic map of the southern third of Louisiana flared to life on a wall screen. "The Air Force will let us off near Baton Rouge. From there, we'll convoy north until this point where we'll turn due west and enter the Atchafalaya Swamp, trading vehicles for Zodiacs that will be waiting for us. Our objective is only a few miles away." He traced the route with a laser pointer. "If we get lucky, alligators won't bite through the rafts and sink them."

"Night operation?" David asked.

Roy nodded. "You know me too well. That's the biggest wetland area in the US, and there are some moderate stretches of open water. The moon's in a dark phase, which will help conceal us."

"Will Milton be hands-on for this one?" David asked.

"Yes. He and Honor should be at Barksdale when we get there. It cut their R&R a bit short, but Milton wouldn't miss it for the world."

Charity stifled a grin. There it was again. Deployment fever. Milton was cut from the *gotta get up close and personal whenever danger strikes* mold, just like his men.

"What happens after we get there?" Glory asked, interrupting Charity's train of thought.

"You'll get your final briefing at Barksdale," Roy replied.

Because she was watching Tony, Charity saw him exchange a brief look with Frank. What was that about? She sharpened her gaze and tried to push into the men's minds, but they sensed her and guarded their thoughts. Frank raised his amber eyes to hers and spoke into her mind. *"Relax. Nothing to concern yourself with."*

"If that's true, then why do I feel like a mule kicked me in the guts?"

"Enough." He drew his dark brows together into a both a warning and a frown.

"Get moving," Roy ordered. "Now. Flight line as soon you can get there."

"What about the Maine site?" David asked as he got to his feet.

"That's classified," Roy replied in a closed-off tone.

Charity dropped the remains of her meal into a trash can and headed for the door, determined to waylay the men once they were outside. Never mind she didn't want anything to do with Tony. She had to find out if they were hatching up something malevolent behind everyone's backs. Something that could send her right back to a compound.

She waited from a vantage point fifty yards from the building. Once they emerged, she plotted a collision course. "Hey!" She planted herself in front of them.

"Hey, what?" Frank sounded annoyed. "We don't have much time."

Charity switched to telepathy. *"What was that look about back in the room. The one you sent Tony's way after Roy said he wasn't going to give us our final orders until we were in Louisiana."*

"Why does it worry you?" Frank countered.

Charity sucked in a breath, undecided if she should toss her cards on the table. A minute ticked by, and the men turned to leave. *"Wait!"* She grabbed Tony's arm. *"It worries me because you might still be working for our kin, and I don't want you to do anything to jeopardize me or the other women's places here at Langley. I'll die before I return to a compound."*

There. She'd said it. Charity stared defiantly at Frank and Tony. She'd have crossed her arms beneath her breasts, but she was still hanging onto Tony.

"Jesus, you're hyper-reactive." Frank all but bared his teeth at her. *"The humans don't trust us. That's all the look was about. They're not telling us the endgame because they're concerned Tony or I will rat them out, and they'll walk into a trap. It's the same reason Roy didn't elaborate about the stealth bombing they have planned for the Maine compound."*

"How do you know about that?" she asked. Pausing a beat, she added, *"You can't be sure because Roy didn't say anything."*

Tony jumped into the conversation. *"He saw it in Roy's head. So did I, for that matter."*

"Charity." Tony laid a hand over the one she still had on his arm. *"You're not thinking. Frank and I can't go back. Not after spilling the location of our headquarters. You think the V4s don't know exactly where that intel came from? Never mind we killed some of our own back in West Virginia."*

She heard truth in his words, and the worry that had turned her belly into a hard knot of fear unwound. "Thanks." She pulled her hand from under Tony's. "Gotta hurry. If we're late, it'll just add to their conspiracy theory fears."

Tony's mouth twisted into half a grin. "Good point. See you on the flight line."

Charity spun and raced toward the building where her

apartment was. Thank fucking God she'd stopped and spoken with the men. There were so many things to worry about, so much that could go wrong, it felt good to have eliminated at least one variable.

Her fingers were still warm from Tony's touch. She wondered what his hand would feel like under her clothing and then shut down that line of thought. Just because Frank and Tony had been forthright with her now didn't make Tony good partner material. He was still a Nameless One.

And he always would be.

She ran harder. Maybe if she really pushed it, the desolate place deep inside her would go away. What the fuck? She was a machine, and machines couldn't feel.

If that's true... She rubbed her breastbone. *Why does my heart ache?*

CHAPTER 4

Tony wiped sweat from his forehead. His clothes stuck to him beneath the Kevlar vest, and he remembered why he hated the Deep South. Even in February, it was humid and buggy, but not overly warm. He swatted at the millionth mosquito with its proboscis aimed for his neck, but it got him anyway.

Frank grunted something unintelligible as they waited for the chopper that would leave them on the outskirts of Baton Rouge.

Tony didn't care much for the plan Milton had outlined. As promised, he and Honor arrived at Barksdale before the jet carrying the rest of them. After listening carefully and making certain Milton was done, Tony raised his hand and waited for permission to speak. Aiming for a neutral, non-argumentative tone, he mentioned the probability of traveling better than eight miles in Zodiac rafts without losing at least one raft to either an alligator or a cottonmouth's fangs was less than two percent.

Milton adopted one of his patronizing looks and asked exactly what Tony was suggesting. When he said they should have at least one extra raft, preferably two, Milton snapped he'd *take it under advisement.*

Tony figured that meant no. Apparently Milton and the boys had done some time in the Okefenokee Swamp in Georgia and hadn't lost any rafts. A veteran of the Vietnamese jungles, with their Mangrove swamps, Milton had likely dealt with his share of crocodiles and poisonous snakes. It was years ago, though. Perhaps the immediacy of death stalking you from all quarters had faded.

Maybe not. If Tony read him right, Milton welcomed danger with a bring-it-on attitude. Every CIA operative he'd met was cut from the same cloth. In a backhanded way, they reminded him of the V4s—aggressive as hell.

A big helicopter—one of the double rotor models—came into view and settled onto the tarmac. Tony squinted against dust from the rotor wash and tightened the strap securing his assault rifle to his shoulder. He was loaded down with so much crap, it'd be a miracle if he didn't end up dead. Because of his genetic alterations, he was used to going into situations light. Just him and his augmented brainpower—when he went at all. In truth, he'd spent most of the last seven years staring through the eyepieces of a microscope or at a computer screen.

The thirty-five pound field pack and heavy rifle, never mind the equally clunky sidearm and two lethal knives, would only get in his way. Using weaponry was far from second nature. By the time he levered a knife loose, or dragged his gun from its holster—or his rifle off his shoulder—whatever had its sights on him would've already struck.

Frank elbowed him. "Maybe it won't be as bad as you think."

Tony clenched his jaw in a tight line and pointed at the chopper. "We're loading. Let's get this over with."

IT WAS WELL past dusk when they stood on the banks of the Atchafalaya Swamp, waiting. The Navy was late delivering the rafts, but plenty of night remained. Clammy darkness settled around Tony, the air thick and fragrant with the odors of vegetation. The chittering cry of a nighthawk, intent on its prey, filled his ears, and he looked up in time to see the bird sweep past, a few feet over his head. Last time he'd been here had been high summer, and the smells weren't nearly as pleasant. Flowering shrubs had mingled with undernotes of rot from the ever-present heat and humidity.

He'd tried to secure a private moment with Charity, but she sat next to Honor in the jet and across from Faith in the chopper. She'd grabbed his arm, though. Not Frank's, but his, when she waylaid them on the Langley campus. And she hadn't pulled away when he placed his hand atop hers. He wished he fully understood her concerns about him. Was it just because he was a Nameless One? Even though he hadn't believed how they treated the women was right, he didn't stand up for them, either.

Maybe if he apologized…

The unmistakable *clack* of alligator jaws snapping shut drew his attention. *Fuck!* He might not have a chance to apologize. Without bothering to run the odds of how well he'd be received, he made his way to where Milton, Roy, and Charlie huddled in a small group. "Hear that?" he asked.

Milton narrowed his eyes. "Of course I heard it. This is a swamp. Swamps in this part of the country have alligators."

"Cottonmouths too." Tony refused to back down. "Their fangs are just as lethal to rubber rafts as anything an alligator can dish out."

"Shit! Are you still on that kick?" Milton's nostrils flared with annoyance.

"Yes, I'm still *on that kick*." Tony struggled to keep sarcasm from leaking into his voice. "Every single time I've been here, I listened to radio reports of lost rafts. Do you know how quickly alligators can immobilize a body before they move in for the kill? Or how fast a cottonmouth's bite can kill?"

"Maybe he's got a point," Roy said. "It won't cost us much to float an empty raft behind us."

"What?" Milton spun to face him. "You've turned into a pussy too?"

Roy straightened his shoulders. "If I didn't work for you, I'd demand an apology. My courage didn't take a hike, but I finally have something I care about living for." He glanced at Glory. "Frankly, I'm surprised you don't feel the same way. Honor could end up a widow before she's even a bride."

"Fine." Milton's expression didn't match his words. "If our friends in the Navy bring more than the two rafts I requested, we'll take a third, and now I'm done with this topic."

Tony inclined his head and walked back to where he'd left Frank.

"Nice work," the other man said softly.

"Hell, I'm a guy, and I'm choking on a surfeit of testosterone. You wouldn't think it'd be so hard to pound sense into those bastards." Tony made a sound between a grunt and a snort and shook his head. "We can deal with animal attacks much more effectively than normal humans, but Milton almost blew the whole thing off. Speaking of which, are you good with us splitting up? I'll go in the raft with Charlie and the women, and you can go with Roy's team."

Frank shot a speculative glance his way. "We're not splitting up, for a whole bunch of good reasons." He paused for a beat. "Still got the hots for her, huh?"

Tony worked his way around Frank's question. "Even if she doesn't want me, I'll still do what I can to make certain she doesn't end up alligator bait. Or worse, captured by our kin at the compound."

"She did seem more worried about that than anything." Frank spoke thoughtfully. "I suppose if I were in her shoes, I'd feel the same way. We really did hand the women a raw deal."

"I'm surprised to hear you say that."

Frank shrugged. "We weren't free to say a lot of things. Hey! I hear a big truck approaching. Bet it's the Navy with those rafts."

"About time," Tony muttered. So far he was less than impressed with human military operations. They could use men like him and

Frank at the helm. Everything would run a whole lot smoother. Frank was smart to veto them splitting up. Tony had been worried about protecting Milton, Roy, and Roy's team, but since their boat would be behind, they'd benefit from whatever threats the lead boat identified and dealt with.

The large truck ground to a halt. Khaki-colored canvas covered its flatbed deck. Tony joined the others milling behind the vehicle, more than ready to snap up the rafts so they could leave. There had to be at least three, perhaps even four, rafts, judging from the way the canvas draped. Tony blew out a tense breath. Additional rafts were necessary from his perspective. The only reason the their kin got away with maintaining a major research center so close to densely inhabited south central Louisiana was because of the Atchafalaya Swamp. Parts of it were rumored to house restless spirits lying in wait to snare the unwary and turn them into dinner for the alligators. Voodoo and other bad mojo were still alive and well in local legends. Not that he actually believed that shit...

A shiver tracked down his back; Tony felt like an idiot. None of that black magic garbage was real, but he could swear he felt something not particularly friendly lurking in the velvety darkness. More snapping jaws brought him back to reality, and he moved forward to help two Navy grunts unload the rafts. There were indeed four of them, but only three had electric motors.

He turned to Roy as they carried a raft to the water. "Can we bring all of them?"

"The one without a motor won't do us much good."

"It has oars," Tony said quietly. "If it's the only game left in town, we'll be glad to have it."

Roy gave a terse nod. "All right. Rope these two together, and I'll take care of the other pair. How the hell did you get in here before?"

"Carefully. Plus freaks from the compound designed specialized boats with hard hulls to navigate these waterways. And they developed an ultrasonic device that sends out a signal to discourage anything living from getting too close."

"Why didn't you say something earlier?" Roy muttered as they lowered the raft into the water and tied it to a stout piece of curved rebar stuck into a concrete pier block.

Tony opened his mouth to say he had, but decided reminding Roy he could've rethought things back at Langley wasn't especially wise. They were here with what they had, and they needed to make the best of it.

Charlie moved past him, followed by the women. They settled into one Zodiac along with Frank. Tony waded through knee-deep murky water to get them away from the bank before slithering into the raft. He double checked the knots securing their Zodiac to the one floating behind them and gave Charlie a thumbs-up sign.

The electric motor sputtered to life, and they glided silently over black water through a forest of submerged Cypress stumps. Occasional curtains of Spanish moss hung from trees they passed beneath. The drone of insects was continuous, and after the hundredth mosquito bite, Tony stopped swatting at them.

"Once we're within sight of the compound," Charlie spoke softly, but even the muted tones held an echo-y quality, and he lowered his voice still further, "we'll work on that mass hypnosis strategy."

"I still don't think it'll work," Frank said. "There are too many of them. This compound holds nearly four hundred. All men. At best, we might knock out a quarter of that number. If they've broken into the Cortexiphan, finished the titration process, and started dosing themselves, our odds will be much worse."

Charlie stood in the boat's stern, piloting it around obstacles. He drew his brows into a frown. "What would you do?"

"Aim for an island near the compound and use grenade launchers to blow the place up with explosives. Wait for the dust to settle and see if we can locate the Cortexiphan, then grab it and leave."

"Tony mentioned that approach back at Langley," Charlie muttered.

Tony didn't say anything. He had floated that idea back at

Langley—along with several others—but Roy shot him down on the grounds it would take too long. He stared at the water, sensing movement beyond the wake from their raft, and dialed his night vision up a few notches.

"Look." He pointed to the port side.

Charity narrowed her eyes. "A bunch of snakes, swimming."

"Cottonmouths." Tony focused his mind and sent a blast of energy into the water. Its dark, slimy surface came alive with movement, but quieted quickly.

"You killed them?" Charlie looked thunderstruck. "Why?"

"They were pacing the raft. It was only a matter of time before they did more than that. They have an exceptional sense of smell. To them we're prey. Nothing more. All they need to do is sink the raft and we're theirs. Don't think they don't know it. People have been boating in these waters forever. Snakes hold archetypal memories—so do alligators."

Frank made an exasperated noise midway between a grunt and a sigh. "I'd forgotten how miserable it was getting to this compound. Sorry. I'll be more vigilant."

"We'll help," Charity said, her voice grim. "I wasn't bothering to scan the water for threats, but I'll start now."

"Us too," Hope, Faith, Honor, and Glory chimed in softly.

"Kill whatever you find," Tony said. "There's not anything in this swamp that wouldn't rather we were dead."

"Back to how we attack the compound," Charlie said. "We do have air support."

"Fine. Have them drop small, targeted bombs," Tony suggested. "We can wait on the island I told you about. As I think about it, that's a more defensible plan, since planes will have better accuracy than we would with grenade launchers."

"Before I radio Milton, are you certain the island's uninhabited?" Charlie asked.

"No," Frank replied. "It was deserted a year ago, but if the compound needed more space, it's a logical expansion site. Level, several feet above the waterline, so it doesn't flood often, and good proximity to the current installation."

Water erupted in a geyser a few feet off their starboard side. Two mangled alligator bodies exploded before sinking beneath the surface. Glory fist pumped the air, and squealed, "Got 'em!"

"Good job, hon!" Honor hugged her.

"Knocks the hell out of trying to be an environmentalist." Hope chortled softly.

"Save your environmentalism for critters that don't want to make a meal out of you," Tony retorted.

Charlie keyed his mike and spoke softly into it. Tony could've listened in, but didn't. The muted hum of the electric motor faded into silence, and Tony understood they'd stopped so the other raft could pull alongside. If they were going to shift gears, they all needed to be on the same page before they left the primary channel and headed into the much narrower passage leading to the compound. At least so far, their chances of discovery by their kin was nil, since this was a fairly busy waterway with frequent swamp tour boats dragging tourists into the Atchafalaya's bayous.

The raft carrying Milton, Roy, and Roy's team chugged next to them, and Roy cut its motor. "We're four point eight miles in," Milton said. "The turnoff into the side channel will come up soon. We need everyone on board with a single plan before we enter that waterway. Now's a good time to remind you we'll be switching to telepathic speech, with communicators as our backup." He shifted position on the pontoon beneath his butt and looked first at Frank then at Tony. "Tell me again why the plan we all agreed on won't work."

"I never agreed with it," Tony said, keeping his voice even.

Milton eyed Roy. "You never told me you didn't have consensus."

"Thought I did. Frank and Tony voiced concerns, but I assumed they got over them."

Milton set his jaw in a tense line. "Talk," he shot at Frank.

"The plan won't work because there are too many of them and

not enough of us. We might be able to hypnotize a hundred, but not four times that number. While we were fighting our way through the other three hundred, we'd have to redirect our mental energy, and the hundred we'd subdued would awaken and join the fight."

"I get it," Milton said. "What's this about an island?"

Tony hastily mapped out Plan B. "We should know damned quick if the island's still deserted. If it's not, there might be other places we could wait out an aerial attack. At least it'll slow the alligators and snakes down."

"How so?" Roy asked.

"They hate high frequency sound waves. It'll drive them into their dens."

Milton tapped keys on his wrist computer, and a map of the swamp flared to life on the tiny display. He leaned toward Tony. "Where's this island?"

Tony pushed between Charity and Hope and studied the map. "Here." He pointed. "If it's not viable, this one back here should be. It's hard to get to because the submerged timber's quite thick, but this is winter, and the water's high because they had an unusually wet year, so we should be able to manage."

"Why not just wait out an aerial attack right here?" Honor asked.

"I want to be close enough to kill any of those fuckers who try to escape," Milton growled.

"If we're at the head of the waterway that leads to their compound, wouldn't we be certain to catch them?" Charity asked.

"Not necessarily," Frank broke in and moved to where he could touch the mapping display. "See this channel? And that one? Both of them make their way back to the main waterway a few miles north. If I were on the run, I'd take the back door route, not the primary one, especially if someone just bombed the shit out of my home."

"We'll head for the island," Milton said. "Total silence. Before we enter the side waterway, I'll radio the pilots and give them an ETA for a strafing run."

"Be sure to key a code when we're in position," Roy cautioned.

Milton shot him a disgusted look. "I didn't just fall off a turnip truck. I understand we may run into unexpected delays. I want them upstairs and ready to rock, but not so close they tip off whoever's monitoring alert systems at the compound."

"Thank you." Tony met Milton's dark gaze across the black pontoons.

"Don't mention it. I have a funny way of listening to my men—especially when what they say makes sense. Get moving. I'll be a hundred yards behind you."

Tony didn't particularly want to go back to his side of the raft. It was nice being sandwiched between Charity and Hope. Even nicer, Charity hadn't drawn away from him. She could have; there was room on her other side. He wanted to talk with her, but this wasn't the time.

"Back to watching for wildlife," he cautioned and made his way to the other side of the raft.

Milton hadn't been kidding about the side channel being close. Within minutes, Charlie guided the Zodiac hard right beneath thick clusters of hanging Spanish moss. The submerged trees grew closer together, and Charlie motioned for Glory to join him. "I need your night vision."

"Telepathy," Frank reminded everyone.

The channel grew progressively narrower. When Tony peered at the vegetation growing on both banks, he groaned inwardly. It was too overgrown to navigate without a machete or taking to the trees. The few times he'd been invited to this compound, he'd never cared for the journey. The Atchafalaya was damned claustrophobic, especially here. By comparison, the channel they'd taken from where they picked up the rafts was a cakewalk, alligators and all.

As if he'd summoned it with his thoughts, a black, triangular head broke the water a few feet away. Tony focused energy to kill it, but the alligator kept on swimming. *What the fuck?* He hit it with higher voltage, gratified when it jackknifed upward and sank amid clusters of bubbles and clanking jaws.

Sharp hissing rose from behind him. It took a second to register; then he forgot all about telepathic speech. "The raft's going down," he shouted. "Into the other one. Now."

Tony lurched around Charlie and dragged the second boat close enough for the women to crawl from one to the other. The alligator who'd likely punctured their raft stuck his head above the waterline; malice sparked from his dark eyes. Tony blasted him, enjoying the surprised look on his reptilian snout when his body separated from his head.

"Go!" Tony snapped, and Frank scrambled into the raft that wasn't sinking.

"Now you!" Charlie pushed Tony forward and followed him into the intact boat.

The first Zodiac developed a definite cant and was taking on water fast. Tony untied the rope linking the two boats. Not much point dragging the sinking raft behind them. It would just snag on all the underwater debris.

Charlie fired the motor, and they lurched forward. "Crap! Good thing we had another raft. Let's try real hard not to lose this one."

"I was scanning." A tremor in Charity's voice revealed how rattled she was. "I didn't sense alligators anywhere close."

"So was I," Glory said. "Same result. No alligators. Shit! That's downright creepy. Do you suppose they're shielded somehow?"

Tony considered it. *"Back to telepathy,"* he instructed. *"Yes, that's exactly what I think. We're close enough to the compound, it wouldn't surprise me if what we're running into are genetically modified alligators, designed especially to protect the compound. It's likely why it took twice the power I thought it should to kill one."*

"Could they do the same thing with snakes?" Charlie asked.

"Of course," Frank replied. *"If something's alive, we can alter its genetic structure."*

"The good news," Tony countered, *"is I can probably figure out a method—or a frequency—to enable communication with them. If we created those fuckers, there has to be a way."*

Charlie glanced at his wrist computer and punched a few buttons. *"We're only a mile out. Shouldn't take but a few minutes to find that other side channel that leads to the island."*

A low buzz tickled the edges of Tony's sensitive hearing. He heard Frank's sharply indrawn breath just before the blackness ahead of them erupted in an explosion that showered them with gallons of the putrid slime that passed for water.

CHAPTER 5

Charity was thrown into the bottom of the boat. At least the fucking thing was still floating.

Faith landed on top of her. "Don't swallow any of that water," she cried.

Charity had already inhaled plenty. Nothing she could do about it now. One thing was abundantly clear, if they ever held the element of surprise, it was long gone.

Water filled the raft to the top of the pontoons, and Charlie shouted, "Look in the aluminum box butted against the bow. Should be a hand pump inside."

Frank pulled it out and started pumping, but it was obvious the pump hadn't been designed for anything this catastrophic.

"I'm taking us to that indentation in the bank." Charlie angled the definitely sluggish raft to starboard. We've got to dump the water out."

"The boat's too heavy," Tony said. "And the bank will be alive with snakes and alligators."

"You have a better idea?" Charlie didn't alter course. "Let's hear it."

"Yeah, turn around," Frank said. "I'll keep pumping. It'll help some. When we get to a wider spot, we'll have better maneuverability."

"What about the Cortexiphan?" Glory asked.

"Could we have choppers land us after the Air Force bombs the place?" Charity asked.

"We could do lots of things," Charlie said grimly, "but those aren't our orders." He reached the bank and keyed his communicator, probably to alert Milton and Roy. The other boat came into view and drew alongside.

"Fuck!" Milton took in Frank and the woefully inadequate hand pump. "What'd you run into?"

"Submerged charge, probably linked to a motion detector hanging from one of those trees," Tony said and swept an arm wide to encompass the sides of the canal. "I had no idea they were here, probably because they were deactivated when we came through these waters on official freak business." He rolled his eyes, probably not liking the label any better than Charity or any of the rest of them.

"You're down to one raft," Milton said and tossed a dour smile Tony's way. "Thanks for being persistent about redundancy."

"Anytime." Tony mock-bowed from his place on the partially submerged pontoon.

"That can't be the only hidden explosive," Charlie muttered.

"Hell no, it's not." Frank looked up from pumping and bit off the next set of words, but Charity saw them in his head. He'd been about to call Roy and Milton brain-damaged for how they designed this mission.

Charity wrapped her arms around herself. The dunking had felt halfway welcome when it happened, but a breeze plastered her wet clothes against her body, and she shivered. It was one thing to attack on foot. Quite another to be at the mercy of this godforsaken, fucking swamp. She wanted to go home and recognized with a jolt that home meant Langley.

When the hell had that happened?

"Alligator!" Hope yelled. "Port side."

When Charity looked, fear bit deep. Alligators was more like it. Half a dozen of the dark, triangular heads cut through the water straight for them.

Tony's energy jolted into her mind as he linked them all. *"One, two..."*

She pushed as much as she had in tandem with the other women, Tony, and Frank, who'd stopped bailing. The lead alligators blew up, spattering them with blood, bits of bone, and clods of tissue, but more swam behind them.

"Get down!" Milton shouted just before the retort of his assault rifle cut through the night. His next words sounded garbled through the ringing in Charity's ears. "The bastards know we're here. No reason for stealth now. I'm radioing the planes. We'll figure out our next steps after they bomb the living shit out of that compound."

Charity heard him relay their coordinates while she kept an uneasy eye on the shadows that had disgorged the alligators. Were there more of them? There practically had to be.

Something brushed against her leg in the murky water that still filled the bottom of the boat. Thinking it was a piece of vegetation— or alligator parts—she dipped her hand beneath the surface and found scales covering an undulating body.

"Shit!" She shot to her feet, hoping to hell her boots were thick enough so whatever was under there couldn't bite her. "Snakes. Snakes in the boat."

Tony bolted upright and scooped her into his arms. "High frequency," he ordered. "Link to my high frequency sound waves and amplify them. It'll drive the snakes to the surface, and then we can kill them."

"Too late!" Frank yelled. The left pontoon's deflating. One of the fuckers must've sunk its fangs into it."

"Kill them anyway." Tony said grimly. "Otherwise, they'll do the same thing to the other two boats." He set Charity down so her booted feet rested on the intact pontoon. "Jump to the other raft. You too." He gestured to the rest of the women.

"Not until the snakes are dead," Honor gritted. "They're showing themselves. Let's do this."

The air took on a glistening edge in response to the combined high frequency sound waves. Snake heads surfaced all around Charity, and she stared, mouth agape. She'd never seen any kind of pit viper up close and personal. Cottonmouths were unsettling in their ugliness, with huge mouths and fangs designed for dealing death. The snakes writhed in death throes, their mouths opening and closing spasmodically before Frank and Tony hefted them into the black water outside the sinking raft.

"Christ!" She scrambled for balance on the pontoon that canted at an increasing angle as the raft sank deeper into the swamp. "I had no idea they were so big. That last one must've been three feet long."

"Get in the boat behind ours," Roy instructed. "Now."

Sound waves from an explosion rocked them, and Charity dove for the relative safety of one of the intact rafts, followed by the other women.

"At least something's going right," Milton muttered. He glanced at his watch and counted down. "Three, two..." His last word was obliterated by more explosions. "One more set should do it." Words crackled through Milton's communications device, but Charity was too rattled to listen.

Milton asked a question or two and then glanced at Frank, last to leave the sinking raft once the snake problem was dispatched. "I just heard from the pilots. That island was still deserted, and they couldn't find any other concentrations of body heat outside the compound."

"Smart to hunt for other places the freaks might be," Tony muttered.

Despite the seriousness of their situation, Charity swallowed a smirk. Tony's tone made it clear he was surprised by anything approximating intelligence coming from normal humans. For the first time ever, a sense of pride for what she was bloomed inside her.

"What's next, boss?" Charlie asked as he joined Milton, Roy, and Roy's team in their boat. Everyone else was in the extra raft tied to it, the one without a motor.

"I'd like to press on," Milton said, "but it doesn't make sense. Just because we wiped out the compound doesn't mean whatever electronic devices the freaks planted in this swamp aren't still active."

Charity blew out a tense breath. She'd been petrified they were going to forge through the overgrown swamp on foot. Vegetation was so thick, she'd never see snakes—or alligators, or whatever other unpleasant surprises lived in this gloomy forest—until they attacked. Although she was loathe to admit it, snakes gave her the creeps. It wasn't logical, but there was something deeply disturbing about their undulating bodies and single-minded assassin mentality.

That's what we are, she reminded herself. *Assassins.*

Killing is killing no matter what kind of righteous banner I hang over it.

She chewed her lower lip, frustrated by her thoughts. Philosophy was uncharted terrain, not a place she was programmed to go.

More explosions sounded from up the waterway, followed by a different kind of detonation. "Goddammit!" Milton punched a closed fist into his hand. "That was one of our fighter jets going down."

Charity peered skyward, but couldn't see a thing through the thick canopy of trees. A series of blasts followed, and Milton keyed his communicator. After a tense exchange, he said. "Pilot punched out. He has our location, and we're going to wait for him."

"How far away is he?" Tony asked.

"Half a mile." Milton's face was set in harsh lines. "He'll make it."

"Give me his coordinates." Tony got to his feet.

"Why?" Milton didn't bother to mask his suspicion.

Tony made his way to the bow of Milton's boat. "I'm going to help him. I can sense things he can't." Tony straightened his spine, standing tall. "No matter how competent that pilot is, he hasn't had the injections, so he's operating with straight up human ability. It's not going to be enough to get him through this swamp." When Milton didn't say anything, Tony pressed on. "You don't trust Frank and me. The thing you don't get is we don't totally trust you, either, but we joined up with you because you were the best alternative. It was a one-way street. We can't go back.

"I'm not keen on bushwhacking my way through that shit." He waved an arm in the direction of the overgrown swamp. "But I'm willing to help save that guy's life. Your call." He crossed his arms over his chest, waiting.

Charity struggled with more unfamiliar emotions. She felt proud of Tony. And worried for him too. Without running their probability of success because she was afraid she'd lose her courage, she got to her feet. "If you go, I'm coming too. We'll be faster as a team."

"The hell—" Tony sputtered.

"I didn't ask you." Charity cut him off and skewered Milton with her gaze, daring him to take a chance on them.

Milton glanced from one to the other. "Done. The pilot went down at—" he rattled off a string of coordinates that Charity filed into her eidetic memory banks. "He'll track as straight a line as he can for us, but—"

"I get it," Tony spoke over Milton. "We'll find him. We have resources you don't. Are the fly boys done?"

"Good point." Milton exchanged a few terse words via his communicator. "Yes. They say there's nothing left to bomb, and they're on their way back to Barksdale." He stopped to take a breath. "While you're gone, we'll rescue the motor from the other raft, so we'll have two functional watercraft."

Charity made her way to Tony's side and eyed the expanse of black water between them and the bank.

Milton must've read her thoughts because he said, "Let me nose the raft up against the bank. At least that'll save you getting wet to your knees."

Charity didn't bother to point out she was already soaked clear through to her underwear, or that when she looked at the water, all she imagined were swarms of hungry cottonmouths lying in wait.

CONFLICT RAGED THROUGH TONY; he pushed it aside because he needed a clear mind. A feral, primitive part of him was filled with joy Charity volunteered to go with him, but a bigger part wanted to order her back to the relative safety of the boats.

"I'm going with you, and that's final," she said next to his ear and pushed energy to sever a tangle of vines blocking their path.

Wondering what else she might have gleaned from her trip through his head, Tony considered shielding his thoughts, but decided it wasn't worth the trouble. Maybe it would be good if she saw the depth of his caring and concern because it might soften her heart toward him.

"Keep those high frequency sounds online," he said gruffly. "It's the best defense we have against things we can't see."

"I hadn't considered shutting them down." She wove her energy more tightly with his.

He assessed the impenetrable undergrowth. They'd made it fifty feet in the ten minutes since they left the shoreline. Not far, but thickly growing vines, trees, and ground cover surrounded them, blocking their vision for more than a few feet. At this rate, it would take hours to cover half a mile, assuming they moved in a straight line, which wasn't looking likely.

"Seventeen point six hours to be precise," Charity said, turning to stare at him. "One way."

"What?" he sputtered. "You've taken up residence in my head?"

"It's hard not to hear your thoughts when you're right next to me. You were thinking it'd take hours, and I simply did the math, but my estimate presumes a steady rate of progress, which we might not manage."

Tony grinned. "Yes, but the pilot is moving toward us. If he covers half the distance—"

Charity held up a hand. "Stop. This is starting to feel like the word problems in those online math classes the Nameless Ones insisted we take."

A warm glow started in his belly at the easy camaraderie between them. He gazed at a bramble thicket blocking their path, and the glow faded a little. Lots of real estate to cross. If they got truly lucky, the animals would give them a break.

"What else lives here?" Charity's voice wasn't as light as it had been when she was bantering back and forth with him.

"Bobcats are our biggest concern, after alligators and snakes. There are some other poisonous ones besides cottonmouths that prefer land to water."

"Peachy." Charity created a path through more brambles with her mind and picked her way through.

They traveled in silence for the next three hundred feet. The farther they got from water, the less he worried about tripping over a stray alligator or tangling with a cottonmouth. The night was alive with the cries of hunting birds and the chittering of small rodents, intent on making it through until dawn intact.

"Do you suppose we should radio the pilot to see how he's doing?" Charity asked after they'd crawled over a fifteen-foot drift of fallen timber. The wood was slick with moisture. Staying on top of the slippery pieces had taken a delicate touch, but they'd wasted time trying to go around it, only to find worse logjams on both ends.

"Never mind," Tony said. "He's pinging me." He keyed his

communicator and noted their coordinates, sharing them with the pilot.

"Fuck!" The pilot cursed. "Still a quarter mile. Never thought I'd blink twice at a thousand feet."

"Keep your guard up," Tony cautioned. "This swamp's not particularly friendly."

"Tell me about it." The other man snorted. "I damn near stepped into a nest of rattlers."

"We'll guide you out," Tony said and cut off communication. It was clear the pilot was anxious and wanted to talk, but they'd get out faster if they kept moving. As it was, Charity was ten feet ahead, walking as fast as she could forge a path by focusing her mind. He hurried after her, intent on getting both of them out of this goddamned swamp so he could tell her how much she meant to him. Even if she didn't return his affection, the least she could do was hear him out.

He sensed a slight alteration in the air currents just before a huge black and tan bobcat soared through the air and landed on Charity's back, driving her to the ground. She screamed, but he couldn't see a goddamned thing once the undergrowth closed over them.

Fear for Charity surged through him, bringing new portions of his augmented brain to life. He located the cat's energy and sent a killing blow spinning toward its heart. Would it be enough? Christ! Had he even hit the fucking thing? His heart beat a tattoo against his ribs. Frantic to get to Charity, he stumbled forward, leaping over bushes and vines blocking his path.

A guttural shriek met his ears, following by a gurgling roar. At least the bobcat wasn't growling or snarling anymore. Was it like the alligators? Genetically modified in some Machiavellian way? They were plenty close enough to the compound for all the predators to have gotten a dose of something to make them more lethal.

"Don't move," he bellowed. "Better if it thinks you're dead."

Even better if it turns on me and leaves you alone.

He practically fell over Charity and the cat since he couldn't see them through thick brush covering the ground. He grabbed the cat, grateful beyond words it was indeed dead, and heaved it off Charity. She groaned, and he bent to push vegetation out of the way. "Don't move," he cautioned, repeating himself. "I need to assess if you're injured."

"I can do that myself," she replied with a dry note that heartened him. Same old Charity, feisty as ever. Thank fucking Christ!

"Did it hurt you?"

"Clawed the crap out of my right shoulder. Other than that, I've got a puncture wound in my left thigh from something I fell on."

"Nothing broken?" he persisted. "Back and neck aren't compromised?"

"For fuck's sake, you sound like a doctor. I told you everything relevant. Now help me up."

Tony gathered her from behind and turned her, so she was on her feet facing him. Because he couldn't help it, he smoothed hair away from her mud-streaked face. "You're so beautiful."

"Don't." She looked away. "We need to keep moving."

"Your shoulder—"

"I already instituted a healing program for it and my thigh. I should be fine."

"This is tender," a voice said from off to their left, "but I've got you in my gun sights. How the fuck did you get away from the compound?"

"You stupid fuck." Tony started to turn toward the voice, but a bullet flashed startlingly close to his head, and he froze.

"No. You're the stupid fuck, and you don't move unless and until I tell you. I lost my plane fighting you bastards. You're lucky I don't gun you down on the spot. Who'd know?"

"You're the pilot we were looking for?" Charity's voice rose in disbelief. "Seems like you'd be a little more grateful we risked ourselves to help you."

"Bullshit! Like I'm going to believe that. You're freaks. No one said jack about freaks coming after me. What'd you do with the rescue party? Kill them?"

The gun's hammer cocked again, the small sound unbelievably loud against all the other noises in the swamp.

Tony judged trajectory and distance. He had to do something, and standing still while trigger-boy shot them wasn't on his agenda.

CHAPTER 6

Charity felt Tony's body tense where it was still pressed against hers. She considered telling him not to kill the pilot, but didn't want to distract him. Clearly, he had something in mind, and if it kept them alive, she was all for it. She'd blown through so much adrenaline already today, she felt raw.

"Don't move. Not a muscle." Tony breathed into her mind.

She swallowed, waiting. There it was. A subtle thrust of energy that flattened the pilot where he stood. She heard him crumple to the ground, heard bushes break under his weight, and was relieved he didn't depress the trigger on his way down. The shot probably would've gone wild, but there was always a chance it could ricochet off something and come back to bite them.

"Fuck!" Charity shook her head to clear thoughts still rattled from the cat attack. "Did you kill him?"

"No, but would you have complained if I did? It's what he planned for us." Tony tilted her chin with a filthy hand and forced her to look at him.

She considered the question. It didn't take long to formulate an answer. "No. He has shit for brains. Maybe he can fly a jet, but he couldn't reason his way out of a tin can."

The corners of Tony's mouth twitched, and a short bark of a laugh rumbled out. "Let's relieve Mr. Pilot of his guns and any knives. Then I'll carry him back to the boats. Unless he comes around before we get there and can move under his own power."

"I feel safer with him out cold. After what he did, we should leave him here. Lots of stuff in this swamp would finish him off damned fast." Charity was surprised by the bitterness in her words.

"We should, but we won't. That'd make us no better than him. Besides, I volunteered to help him, and I will, whether he wants me to or not."

"Yeah huh? It was looking like he'd rather die than accept anything from a freak." She opened her mouth to say more, but clacked it shut. No point mentioning that no matter how much help they offered, most normal humans would never accept them. "How do you want to do this? I can get his arms or legs."

"Nah. I'll just hoist him over a shoulder. You can carry his guns and make the path we created wider if it needs to be."

Charity made her way to the man and pried the pistol out of his hands, careful to set the safety. The pilot looked young, not more than twenty-five. Blond hair was cut close to his scalp, and he had the same lean, mean look she'd come to associate with CIA operatives. His camouflage flight suit had long rips in it, and his hands were scratched and bloody. Tony dragged a second pistol out of its holster and patted the man down, finding a lethal looking hunting knife in a thigh sheath.

By the time she attached the knife and pistols to her body, she felt like an ad for the NRA. "Look at me." She spun in place, listening to metal clank against itself in a discordant symphony. "I'm the envy of every well-equipped terrorist."

"Because of that dynamite body, not the arsenal." Tony's gaze moved over her in a slow, lazy way that pleased and unsettled her. A tongue of heat licked between her legs, and she slammed a barrier around her thoughts. The absolute last thing she wanted was for him to know he turned her on.

Tony grunted as he picked the pilot up and draped him over a shoulder. "Let's get moving. This shouldn't take nearly as long as the trip in."

Charity led the way through trampled down bushes. They had trouble with the fifteen-foot logjam they'd climbed over and managed it by handing the still-comatose pilot from one to the other.

Tony was just hoisting him back over his shoulder when the other man started to come around. He struggled weakly, and Tony dropped him back on his feet, holding him upright, so he wouldn't fall over. "Now you look here," he growled. "You may not like my kind, but we carried you from where you'd have shot us and left us for dead. The boats are only fifty yards away."

The pilot shook his head from side to side blearily. "You really are who the CIA sent to help me?"

"What do you think?" Charity demanded, fighting down anger. "You sorry piece of shit. I risked my life to help you, and what do I get for it?"

"Enough!" Tony's voice cracked like a whip. He returned his attention to the pilot. "Can you walk?"

"Yeah," the man said sullenly. "What the fuck did you do to me?"

"He didn't kill you," Charity gritted out. "And he could have. Get going." She pointed at the obvious path they'd forged. "We'll be behind you."

"Keep an eye out for snakes and alligators," Tony cautioned. "We're close enough to the water for them to be a problem."

Breath whistled from between Charity's teeth. If she never saw another swamp, it'd be too soon. It was tough to believe tourists paid good money to sightsee here.

Honor and Glory met them before they got to the boats. "Damn, but you're a sight for sore eyes." Glory pushed past the pilot and pulled Charity into a hug. "We were worried about you."

Honor stared at the pilot and then at Tony. Narrowing her eyes, she directed her next words at Tony. "Your energy's partially draped around him, so he's still digging his way out of something you did. I'm guessing he gave you problems."

"You might say that," Charity replied. "Watch it, hon. He hates us and would've killed us if Tony hadn't stepped in."

"You were perfectly capable of controlling him," Honor said pointedly.

"Not exactly. I'm not as good at titrating the energy as Tony, and the odds I might have killed that jackass were fifty six point four percent higher. Although, at that point, I wasn't exactly running probabilities." She laughed grimly. "We were just trying to stay alive."

"What happened to your back?" Glory asked, fingering the torn fabric running down Charity's shoulder.

"It's a long story. If it's all the same to you, I want to get out of here more than I've wanted out of anywhere since we escaped from the compounds."

The pilot stood off to one side, taking everything in. Finally, he asked in a choked voice. "Do a lot of you work for the CIA?"

"Why?" Tony asked. "Would you think less of an organization that would hire us?"

Emotion played over the pilot's face, and he seemed to come to a decision. He turned to face Tony squarely. "My name is Gene Riley. I apologize for my behavior when we met. I wasn't at my best, but I don't want to make excuses. I'm hoping we can get off on a better foot. You would've been within your rights to kill me, since you assessed rightly that I was within seconds of offing both of you." He stopped to suck in a breath. "I owe you my life. I wouldn't blame you if you didn't want to, but I'm more than willing to bury the hatchet." He held out a hand, waiting.

Tony made his way to where Gene stood and took his hand, shaking it firmly before letting go. "No hard feelings. We've been at odds for seven years. The animosity won't go away overnight."

Gene broke into a grin. "Thanks. That's more than I deserve. Let's hit those boats. I want to let my wife know the kids still have a daddy. My CO will have called her, but she never relaxes until she hears my voice." He turned and made his way along the path they'd cleared.

"Best suggestion I've heard all day." Charity followed him, still vigilant. Five feet from safety didn't count if an alligator decided she looked like an hors d'oeuvre. She pushed high frequency sound out, joining with Tony, Honor, and Glory. Damn, it felt good to be a part of something with her people.

"We love you too," Glory said.

Charity didn't chide the other woman for helping herself to her thoughts.

"You were gone so long we got worried," Honor cut in, "so I talked Milton into letting us meet you."

"Any word about the compound or the Cortexiphan?" Tony asked from his place at the rear of the group.

"Compound's history. No idea if there were any survivors," Glory replied. "I guess we're going to borrow some choppers from either the Navy or Air Force and go in for a looksee, but not until we've had a few hours' rest."

Rest.

Charity shut her dry, scratchy eyes for a moment. Food and a bed, even one on the ground would be welcome—so long as it wasn't in this godforsaken swamp. Her shoulder ached from the cat's claws. She'd worked to clear any infection, but the three deep gouges were far from healed. The puncture wound in her thigh was doing better, but it hadn't been as deep or done as much damage. She'd chafed at her protected life in the compound, longed for adventure. Maybe not quite this much, though. A laugh bubbled up before she could get a handle on it.

"What?" Tony's deep voice rumbled from behind her.

"Nothing."

"Seriously, what? I'd like to know."

"I was just thinking that I spent hours, days, weeks back at the compound wishing for a different life. One full of exploits, quests."

"Got a bit more than you bargained for, did you?" Warmth ran beneath his words.

"You might say that."

"It's about fucking time." Milton's unmistakable voice blasted her. "I was about ready to call out the cavalry."

"I thought you were the cavalry," Charity retorted.

"If you were that worried, why didn't you radio me?" Tony cut in. "Or use telepathy?"

"He wasn't really worried." Honor trotted to Milton's side and wrapped an arm around his waist. "His bark's worse than his bite."

"Ssht." He sent a pointed look her way. "No giving away my secrets." Milton shifted his focus to the downed pilot. "Welcome, son. We'll see you get home."

"Sir." Gene snapped off a crisp salute. "Appreciate the assistance, sir."

Charity started to tell Milton about Gene's latter day attitude adjustment, but Tony prodded her from behind. *We don't need to say a word. Return his weapons quietly, once we're in the raft.*

"But—"

"He apologized," Tony said. *It's good enough for me.*

TONY STRETCHED full length on the bed in his assigned quarters at the Joint Reserve Naval Air Base. He'd showered, but gotten back into his clothes since he hadn't brought any others. A robe hung in the closet—no doubt for visitors much like him—but he wasn't ready to go to sleep yet.

Their return trip through the Atchafalaya was as smooth as the inbound leg had been rough—with one raft tag-teaming the other— and he couldn't help but believe the compound was responsible for most of their problems. Certainly the obvious ones like the underwater explosion and the alligators and snakes attacking in groups. He'd searched his database brain and discovered reptiles and pit vipers generally worked alone.

The Air Force had shown up to collect Gene, and he'd made it a point to shake Tony's hand once more before leaving, saying again how sorry he was and inviting Tony to dinner if he was ever in the Barksdale area.

Between Roy's team, Milton, and Charlie, they traded drivers on the trip back to the air base, spelling one another when someone felt sleepy. Somewhere along the way, they ran through a burger drive-through. Even though he and Frank were more than capable of driving—as was Glory—none of them had driver's licenses, an omission Milton said he'd take care of once they were back at Langley.

Tony rolled over, but he felt keyed up, not sleepy at all. He could've instructed his mind to enter sleep mode, but what he really wanted was find Charity and talk with her. They'd been in separate cars driving back, and it damn near killed him when Chris shepherded her into his vehicle. Tony hung back while she smiled at the other man, but it took all his self-control not to storm their vehicle, drag Chris out, and smash his face in. Chris may have commando training, and the benefit of the injections, but in a contest of raw strength, Tony would win hands down.

He debated the wisdom of a middle of the night chat with Charity and finally decided the worst thing that could happen was she'd chase him away. Relieved to have come to a decision, he dropped his legs over the side of the bed and flowed to his feet. Each of them had been assigned a room in this building, so finding Charity would be as easy as tracking her energy. He put on his boots —the only shoes he had with him—and laced them.

What if she's with Chris?

Then I'll go away.

Tony stopped midway to the door. Big words, but would he really slink away? Wasn't he just as likely to kick in the door and pound Chris into a pile of dog meat? He winced. If he was going to do a Rambo imitation, he'd be better off staying in his room. After a long, indecisive five minutes, he padded to the door and let himself into the corridor. He searched his floor, but didn't find her.

The building had three stories; his room was on the second. Determined to move forward, he trotted down a flight of stairs, thinking he'd look on the first floor before hitting the third. Partway down a long hall carpeted in industrial beige, he latched onto Charity's energy, and relief raced through him. She was alone. Judging from her energy signature, she was still awake too.

Before he could think it to death, he tapped softly on her door. She'd know it was him if she used her augmented ability. A bigger question was if she'd open the door. He waited, barely breathing, but the latch clicked, and the door slid open an inch or two.

"You may as well come in," she called softly.

Tony slipped through the door. He pulled it shut behind him and walked into a room identical to his own. Twin beds butted against the wall with a window, and a dresser sat catty-corner. The door to the small, utilitarian bathroom opened off to his right.

Charity perched atop one of the beds, with the covers turned down, eying him. "What do you want?" She taken off her field gear and was wrapped in a robe, twin to the one he'd found in his own closet, but hadn't bothered with.

"Mind if I sit down?" He glanced at the other bed.

"Help yourself, but don't plan on staying long. You didn't answer my question. It's been a rough day, and we need sleep."

"You're still awake." He pointed out and perched on the edge of the other bed. Now that it came down to it, he didn't quite know what to say. Should he tell her how he felt? Or would it be better to feel her out before he laid himself bare?

"Look." She exhaled noisily. "I know why you're here. You think you like me, but I can't go there."

"Why not?" He trained his gaze on her, not wanting to miss any clues beneath whatever words she chose to share.

She thinned her lips into a flat line. "I'm surprised you have to ask. I've had a bellyful of Nameless Ones. It wasn't enough that you told me when I could eat, when I could sleep, and rationed every fucking thing I needed to be comfortable." She bolted to her feet and stood over him, hands on her hips. "It didn't stop there. Of course it didn't. You fuckers had to mess with my genome, as if it weren't unstable enough in the first place."

"Charity." He spread his hands in front of him. "They were trying to make it better. Fix their mistakes."

"That's one word for it." She glared down at him. "I can think of lots of others. You experimented on me, goddammit. Those experiments damn near killed me."

"I didn't experiment on you. I worked with Frank to save you once we understood what was happening to your genetic structure."

She threw her hands in the air and tossed her head. "You're splitting hairs. Playing semantics." She pushed loose strands of dark silkiness out of her face, but her curls fell back across her sculpted cheekbones the minute she moved her hands away. "Bottom line is you're a Nameless One. You robbed the other women and me of our humanity. Used us. Saw us as expendable. And now you want me to fall into your arms."

Tony looked away. Everything she said was true, and his role in what the compounds had turned into jabbed him. He may not have agreed with things, but he hadn't taken a stand against the status quo, either.

"When you put it that way…" He got to his feet. "I'd probably feel the same way if our situations were reversed. I am sorry for what happened to you, and for not speaking up about the way we treated our women. Hear me out, and then I'll leave."

She made come along motions with one hand.

He squared his shoulders. This wasn't the time to be anything other than totally honest. "I care about you, Charity. I've fought against it—told myself it was absurd—but I started falling in love with you the night Frank and I saved your life. I was linked to your mind then, and I saw how pure and polished your spirit is. Sure, you've got rough edges, but beneath the bravado, you're kind and thoughtful and courageous. Exactly the kind of woman I want as part of my life."

She opened her mouth, but he held up a hand. "Let me finish. None of the men—me included—have any experience with women. All our breeding occurred in petri dishes, so this is uncharted territory for me too. I understand why you might have a hard time trusting me, but I'm hoping you'll at least consider my offer and give us a chance."

"What offer?" Color splotched across her cheeks. "I've heard a bunch of excuses, but no offer."

"I, um, that is—" He swallowed hard and pushed the rest of his words out. "I'd like to spend time with you. Get to know you better, and let you get to know me."

"What if you decide you don't like me as well as you think you will?" Her green-eyed gaze settled on him. Challenge sparked from her.

He wanted to gather her against him, protect her, reassure he'd take care of her... "Like I said, this is a whole new ballgame—for both of us. I've never dated a woman. Never expected to have the opportunity to share my life with anything beyond my genetics lab."

"At least you're being honest."

Tony took a chance, closed the short distance between them, and wrapped her in his arms. He drank in the clean scents of her body and newly washed hair. "You feel so good against me, Charity." He caressed her shoulders through her borrowed robe. His cock swelled where it was trapped between them, but the sexual jolt was almost secondary, compared with the wonder of the woman in his arms.

For the space between two heartbeats, she hugged him back, but then she stiffened and pushed away. "No matter how good you feel," she said in a choked voice, "you need to leave."

"I don't want to, but I will."

"Yeah." She brushed at overflowing eyes. "That's the problem. I don't want you to leave, either, but I also don't want you to stay. I've never been so goddamned conflicted about anything, and I hate how it makes me feel."

Tony wanted to touch her, soothe her, but something about the way she held herself warned him not to. She had to approach him, not the other way. "I'm sorry for everything the Nameless Ones did to you and the other women. I'll carry guilt for my part in that forever, but I can't change the past."

"That's the dilemma." Her voice was so soft, he had to strain to hear her. "Neither can I. Now go."

Understanding he'd done all he could, Tony let himself out the door. His last glance at her broke his heart. She stood tall, watching him go, with resignation streaming from her in weary waves.

Because he couldn't stand the thought of returning to his room, he went outside and broke into a fast jog. He felt broken, damaged, and truth dawned that the women weren't the only victims of life in the compounds. Maybe Cortexiphan could save them, but the more he thought about it, the more he shied away from any more artificial anything. No more enhancements, no more manipulations. From now on, he'd accept his limitations, not continue seeking perfection. It didn't exist. He'd been chasing a chimera for seven years and run roughshod over countless experimental subjects in the process.

That part of his life was over. Starting now, he'd use his ability to enrich what he and the other genetically altered humans already had, not keep chasing impossible rainbows.

The revelation shocked him, but the possibility of freedom it offered was exhilarating. Drained, but finally ready to lose himself in sleep, he made his way back to his bed.

Charity might not have welcomed him with open arms, but at least she hadn't kicked him out before he told her how he felt. Maybe, just maybe, she'd reconsider and let the spark he sensed between them grow.

CHAPTER 7

Charity watched the door close behind Tony and wrapped her arms around herself. Once he was gone, she allowed tears to fall thickly. A painful lump at the back of her throat made swallowing difficult, and her chest felt like steel bands enclosed it. No matter how much she didn't want to have feelings for Tony, he touched a place inside her that Chris would never get close to.

On the long car ride to the naval base, Chris kept up a steady stream of chatter, feeding her questions. He even placed a friendly hand on her thigh, but stopped short of suggesting they get together that night. She helped herself to his thoughts shamelessly, but she learned a lot. Apparently Chris had a blueprint he followed with women that yielded an almost hundred percent success rate for getting them into bed. He was simply sticking to the same pattern with her. Initiate conversation, appear interested, don't move too fast…

She couldn't wait for the car to leave them off at the base, so she could get away from his carefully choreographed moves. At least Tony had been honest with her—brutally so, but honest. Compared with Chris, he had nada in the way of experience with women and wasn't ashamed to admit it.

She swiped her forearm across her streaming eyes and went to get a length of toilet paper to wipe them and blow her nose. At least Tony would give her space; she'd seen it in his mind. Chris on the other hand, would move blithely to phase two in his "how to conquer women" strategy, but likely not until they were back at Langley.

The next day or two would be full since they'd be picking through the wreckage of the compound. They had to make certain no Cortexiphan was left for the freaks to dose themselves with, otherwise their teams would head straight back to Langley. She wondered if the Maine compound was a smoking ruin too. If this kept up, there wouldn't be any freaks left to request amnesty—even if they wanted it.

She threw the wad of tissue in the trash. Nothing left to do but sleep, so she killed the lights with her mind and crawled into bed. For the barest moment, she let herself relive the feel of Tony's arms around her. His body was hard with corded muscle, but his hands on her back had been gentle. She'd felt his erection against her belly, but he hadn't made the slightest move to follow through, even though she sensed his arousal.

She'd been too flustered and confused to be aroused while he held her, but need flooded her now. His cock had felt huge against her body, the heat from him branding her. His scent, spicy and masculine, still clung to her. She found her swollen clit with her fingers and rubbed in hard little circles until her hips bucked with release. It happened fast, so fast it shocked her. Usually she had to work a little to get herself to come. Not tonight.

Charity made a grab for the momentary lull in her thoughts after her climax and forced her body into sleep mode. Staying alive through the rest of this mission trumped her romantic problems, and she'd be worse than a fool to forget that.

Her programming woke her at five, and she took another shower before getting back into her stinky, sweaty field gear. At least she wouldn't smell any worse than everyone else. Her shoulder was healing; so was her thigh. She rotated her shoulder blade, pleased when her discomfort was minimal.

The plan was breakfast in the mess hall, which she assumed was nearby, at zero five thirty. They'd leave right after that.

"If you're ready, we could walk to breakfast together." Tony spoke into her mind.

Charity froze. She hadn't expected him to approach her again, but her heart fluttered oddly in her chest, and a warm, buttery feeling filled her.

"Charity? I know you heard me. Did I wake you?"

"Yes. No. Uh, yeah I'll meet you outside in five."

"Fantastic! See you then." His enthusiasm was palpable, even in telepathic mode.

"Jesus Christ! What have I done?" she muttered and looked at her field jacket. She probably wouldn't need it for breakfast, or her rucksack, or her guns. After a last look at her gear, she let herself out of her room and made her way to the door at the end of the hallway.

Tony waited for her in darkness giving way to a gray dawn. He didn't try to touch her. Just sent a smile her way that melted her insides.

"Do you know where the mess hall is?" she asked.

He nodded. "I downloaded a map of this place. It's about a quarter mile that way." He pointed, keeping his gaze trained on her. "Will you be warm enough?"

Charity rolled her eyes. "You're kidding, right? It's in the high forties already, and the sun's nowhere near up."

"Feel like a run?"

"Sure." She paced him, enjoying the way their augmented strength lent lightness to their stride. Then she remembered Chris lumbering behind her, panting and complaining she was too fast. No comparison. No way a human could measure up, no matter how much she might want him to.

"Do you know any more about today's plans?" she asked.

"Nothing beyond last night's briefing after we got here," he said, "but I did have some thoughts about Cortexiphan."

"A new use for it?"

He shook his head. "No. I can see continuing to use it for emergencies—like what happened to you when your genetics had a meltdown, but I'm done searching for the perfect version of us. Normal humans have gotten by forever, and they have considerably fewer resources than we do. The only reason we kept trying to make ourselves better was to secure revenge for the breeding farms—"

"And you think we're ready to move past that." She finished for him.

"I don't see any percentage in holding that grudge any longer. It's gotten in the way of us moving forward as a people to do good things—responsible things—with our abilities."

"Normal humans designed us to be warriors."

"True, but they choked on that plan since we took our warrior ability and turned it against them. Something I'm certain they never foresaw." He paused for a beat. "Anyway, that was over seven years ago. A lot has changed since then, and we need to redesign our relationship with them."

Charity drew to a halt. She wanted to finish the conversation and saw the mess hall off to their right. It had to be the right place since it was lit up, and she spied a food line through the windows.

"Do you honestly believe enough of us will be left to make any difference to anyone?" She kept her voice low, rather than switching to telepathy.

He nodded solemnly. "I do. If Milton's boys blew up the Maine compound—and I'm fairly certain they did—that'll make five compounds plus headquarters. We left survivors, but still. No matter how much we resent what normal humans did to us, we're not stupid. I believe we'll start seeing first a trickle and then a flood, as our people seek not just amnesty, but how they can fit into a new paradigm that includes playing nice with humans, rather than hating them."

"I hope you're right." She wrapped her arms around herself. The morning air held a chilly edge she hadn't noticed while they were running.

"Come on." He jerked his chin toward the mess hall. "Let's get coffee and breakfast."

She headed toward the door at the far end of the building with *Enter Here* painted over it, while her mind ran the probability of large numbers of freaks successfully integrating with human culture.

"I already did that." Tony held the door open for her. "Depending on how you design the parameters, it's between forty and eighty-two percent."

She locked gazes with him, enjoying the banked heat in his amber eyes. "You were in my mind."

He didn't bother denying it. "You could've kept me out. You didn't. Do you want cream and sugar in your coffee?" Without waiting for an answer, he walked briskly toward two enormous stainless steel urns.

Charity followed him, deep in thought. Could they simply let go of their animosity toward all things human? When an answer came, it was complex enough she wanted to examine it before she discussed her conclusions with anyone.

TONY NURSED a second cup of coffee while the other women, Charlie, Milton, and Roy and his team took seats at the same table. Charity had the seat across from him, and he stole glances at her from time to time. He didn't need to look at her, though, to lose himself in the glow of her energy. He hadn't known what to expect when he'd taken a chance and invited her to walk to breakfast. That she hadn't told him no outright felt huge. And she'd listened to him, which kindled hope she might be able to overcome her barriers and let herself care about him.

"Flight line at zero six thirty," Milton said. "We want to take advantage of all the daylight we can." He shifted his gaze to Frank and Tony. "Anything we need to know?"

Frank looked up from the scrambled eggs and bacon on his plate. "Depends. How certain are you that everyone is dead?"

"The pilots seemed certain," Roy answered, "and they have heat-seeking technology."

"Yes, but this compound is probably like all the rest," Tony cut in. "It should have underground rooms and corridors shielded with metal. Your heat-seeking devices couldn't read anything through plate steel."

"Are you certain about it having underground rooms?" Milton asked.

"I never actually saw them," Tony admitted, "but the probability is high, since all the compounds were built from a common design." He set his mug down with a *thunk*. "You're asking for a reason. What is it?"

"Two reasons," Milton clarified. "First, we need to be far more cautious if some of your kin are still there. Second, it would be hard to build anything underground in the swamp. Hell, many of the graveyards in this part of Louisiana are aboveground since groundwater seeps into graves dug into the earth."

"Mmph." Frank frowned. "Hadn't thought about that. I never saw any underground rooms when we were there, but it never occurred to me they didn't exist."

"How about this?" Tony suggested. "We'll hunt down the computer, assuming anything's left of it. That'll tell us quick enough, because it'll be in the most protected location they have. If it's aboveground, that means no subterranean tunnels."

"Can you do that from the air?" Charlie asked.

"Sure." Frank nodded. He sent a speculative look Milton's way. "Any chance Tony and I could have our own chopper?"

Milton drew his brows together. "I'm not questioning your ability to link with the craft's computer and fly it, but the liability is enormous since neither of you have any kind of pilot's license. Why can't you go in the two birds with the rest of us?"

"We could." Frank spoke slowly. "If we do it my way, we can actually become an extension of the helicopter. When we join its onboard computer, we'll be much more maneuverable than a normal pilot-chopper combo. The craft will jump to our thoughts, which means we can take bigger risks to find what we need."

"If anyone's left down there, flying up their ass might not be such a good idea," Roy cautioned. "If you get too close, they can blow you right out of the air, and neither of you has any experience punching out of a midair explosion. That maneuver is especially dicey in a chopper because of the rotor."

"Give us some credit." A corner of Tony's mouth twitched into a grim smile. "One of us would fly the bird. The other would keep an eye out for airborne missiles aimed at us. Depending on the flight characteristics of the helicopter, there's roughly a seventy-five percent chance we could avoid being hit." He paused. "We can sense the missile the moment it leaves the ground, which gives us a definite edge."

"Too bad we didn't have you in Vietnam or the Middle East," Milton muttered and got to his feet. "I'll see what I can do about clearing this with the CO here at the base. Catch the rest of you at the flight line with your full field gear."

A chorus of "You got it, sir," ran around the room.

Tony turned to Frank. "Do you think they'll go for it?"

The other man shrugged. "Who knows? I've always wanted to fly one of those things, though."

"Let's think through how this would work," Roy broke in.

"Nothing to think through," Frank replied. "We'll go in and gather intel. Once we have something useful, we'll report back to you. Next moves would be determined by what we find."

"If anyone shoots at us," Tony added, "another of those jets would come in handy. In case the place isn't as empty as we hope."

"Cross that one when we get there," Roy said. "They're all back at Barksdale."

"I was hoping we could assume the Cortexiphan got blown to hell along with the rest of the compound," David muttered.

"We all hope that." Roy glanced at his team member. "It might have, but we can't take a chance without checking. That stuff is too potent to risk leaving it with the freaks."

"What happened at the Maine compound?" Frank asked.

"We have ground teams sorting through what's left today," Roy replied after a silence that stretched so long, Tony was getting ready to call him on it.

"Even after everything, they still don't trust us," Frank said, shielding the communication for just the two of them.

"Maybe not," Tony answered carefully, *"but they're getting closer. It's not like he shined you. Or hid behind saying the information was classified."*

"Don't get too comfortable," Frank warned. *"They're still different from us. And they'll never offer us equal status."*

Tony wasn't certain of that, but he didn't want to get into a mental argument with Frank, so he just nodded and got to his feet. "I'm off to collect my gear. See all of you soon."

CHAPTER 8

Charity bounced against her shoulder harness in the chopper. The air was rough today, and the bird jolted them around whenever they hit an air pocket. The men had gotten their wish and had their own small chopper. She wished she could see them, but she needed to be on the other side of the craft for that.

They were scattered among three helicopters. She and Charlie and the women were in one, and Roy and his team in the second. Milton was flying their bird with Charlie. One of Roy's team was acting as his copilot. It had taken nearly an hour to get into position. They hovered at four thousand feet, waiting for Frank and Tony to fly close enough to tell if the compound's computer was still intact and underground—and if any freaks remained to fight back.

Faith sat on one side of her and Hope on the other. "It'll be good to get this over with," Hope said. "It's not much fun rummaging through dead bodies. I hated the Nameless Ones, but I didn't necessarily want them dead. Just off our backs."

"Look sharp," crackled through Charity's headset right before the craft banked hard right. When she sent power spiraling outward, she sensed ordnance speeding toward them.

"Shit! Aw shit. Frank and Tony," she cried. "Did something hit them?"

"They're okay," Glory said from the other side of the bird.

"More than okay," Honor confirmed. "Wow! Great evasive flying."

"Settles one thing," Charity ground out. "Some of us are still alive and kicking down there."

"I'm opening the outside channel so everyone can hear," Milton said from the cockpit, and static grew louder in Charity's ears.

"No underground room. The computer is in a partially submerged, shielded concrete bunker," Frank reported. "It's still functional, so it's possible that's what's behind the missile that just zipped past."

"More likely some freaks took cover, alongside the computer," Milton said.

"There is a better than eighty percent chance of that, yes," Tony agreed, sounding extraordinarily calm. Charity suspected he was enjoying the hell out of this.

"Normally, I'd have us put down a short distance away and approach from the ground," Milton said, "but that's not possible with the swamp. Nowhere to land, and too hard to make our way to the compound with all the booby traps likely surrounding the place."

"What do you want to do, boss?" Roy's deep voice rumbled through Charity's headset.

"I hate to leave the Cortexiphan, but I'm calling the mission. It'd be suicidal to land."

"Tony and I might be able to get through," Frank said.

"How?" Milton sounded testy.

"Any booby traps would be set to trip for humans, not for us. There's better than a fifty percent chance we could get in there."

Charity bit her lower lip hard enough to draw blood. It was too dangerous. Fifty percent wasn't good enough. She didn't want Tony anywhere near that compound. Who knew how many freaks were left? He and Frank might walk right into an ambush. She held her breath, waiting to see what Milton would do.

After a pause so long she was ready to undo her harness and storm into the cockpit, Milton finally said, "Negative. Too risky. We have no idea what you'd face. Plus, you still have the problem of approach and nowhere to safely land the bird."

"We may have located a landing pad," Frank said. "I see a spot not all that far from the compound. It's big enough for us—barely."

"No." Milton snapped off the word. "All craft return to base. We'll figure out something else."

Charity exchanged a worried glance with the other women. Frank and Tony were just as likely to charge ahead with their own agenda as they were to heed Milton.

"It'll be okay, hon." Faith patted her leg.

"Yeah, give the men a little credit," Hope said. "Neither of them have a death wish."

Charity's helicopter banked into a climbing turn to gain altitude.

She stared out the windows, willing both other craft to follow. Her heart hammered against her ribs. The chopper that was twin to theirs came into view, but not the smaller bird with the men. "Do you see them?" she asked Honor and Glory. "They were on your side."

Honor twisted in her seat so she could look down. "No. Yes! There they are, and they're gaining elevation."

"Thank fucking God." Charity pulled air deep into her lungs, willing herself to calm down.

"No kidding," Honor said. "I still remember those hours when I was certain Milton was dead. Worst time I've ever spent, mostly because we had a big misunderstanding, and I hadn't had an opportunity to tell him how sorry I was. Thinking I'd lost my chance to apologize damn near killed me."

Charity gazed at her hands. Would she feel the same way if something happened to Tony, and she'd held back because of him being a Nameless One?

"I know what you're thinking," Glory said and pulled off her headset. "No reason for the men to hear any of this."

Charity yanked her headset off and turned the transmit switch to off. The other women followed suit. "What?" She looked from one to the other. "Is this where I get a whopping dose of well-meaning chick advice just like in the movies?"

"Yup." Glory grinned at her. "It is."

"Kind of like the blind leading the blind." Honor smiled too. "It's not like any of know all that much about men or relationships. Not really."

"You know what they used to say back at the compound," Faith said. "See one, do one, teach one."

"Yeah and look how well that worked out." Hope reached across Charity and jabbed Faith in the ribs.

"Regardless," Glory said and focused her green eyes on Charity. "We all know you're interested in Tony."

"How could you possibly know that?" Charity sputtered. "Unless you've been eavesdropping on my thoughts. Or Honor blabbed."

"Maybe we know because we have eyes," Glory countered. "In any event, if the only thing holding you back is that he's a Nameless One, you might want to reconsider."

"I second that thought." Honor jumped in quickly, before Charity could say anything. "He's not one of the ones who made our life hell."

"Maybe not," Charity said. "That would fly better, except he's all but admitted he didn't do shit to stand up for the women at his compound."

"Does he feel bad about it?" Hope asked.

Charity nodded slowly. "At least he says he does."

"Well, is he telling the truth?"

"Yes. I checked."

"So what's the problem?" Glory asked. "You like him. He likes you. He feels guilty about the way the compounds were run. If it were me, I'd give him a chance."

"You would?" Charity stared at her, thinking she must've heard wrong.

"We all would," Honor said. "It's a lonely life we led. I'm appreciating the hell out of Milton. I had no idea what I was missing. And it runs way deeper than sex, by the way."

"What Honor said." Glory reached across the narrow aisle to pat Charity's hand. "I had my doubts about linking myself to a normal human, but Roy is just such a stellar guy, I've never looked back."

"He's pretty danged hot on top of all that," Hope said wistfully.

"So's Milton." Faith blushed and turned to Charity. "Hope and I would kill to find men. We think you're lucky someone you like is attracted to you."

Charity glanced from one to the other and managed a deadpan grin. "Isn't anyone going to go all gaga over how hot Tony is?"

Honor cocked her head to one side. "All the Nameless Ones are hunks. It's their genetics. That part of *let's create perfection* worked out just fine."

Charity smiled in spite of herself. "I've been thinking about lots of things lately. Our relationship with our own men—and with normal humans too. Both those equations have shifted since the night we were rescued from our compound."

"I suppose it's good you're thinking things through." Glory winked at her and settled back against her hard seat. "I wouldn't waste too much time on where we fit into the normal human hierarchy, though. Not yet anyway, because it's still in flux. I'm going to try to get some sleep. Roy kept me up most of last night."

Hope rolled her eyes and reached across the narrow aisle to punch her. "Brag about it, why don't you?"

"Just stating facts, sister. We're machines. Facts are where we live."

The good-hearted banter continued, but Charity tuned it out. She had some decisions to make. Because she didn't know any other way, she started running probabilities.

~

TONY LAID his hand on the cyclic. "I'll take the chopper for a while."

"I still think we should turn around and go for it," Frank muttered, withdrawing from the craft's computer system.

"I do too, but that's not how normal humans do things—at least not normal humans locked into a military chain of command. You're correct that they don't totally trust us yet. If we follow our own plan—in direct opposition to orders we were given—they never will." Tony glanced across the cockpit.

"Point taken, but I hate to leave when we're so close to the Cortexiphan."

"We don't need *this* batch of Cortexiphan since we can synthesize what we need from lab supply firms, now that we finally have access to them."

"Yeah, but we have to get it away from whatever freaks are left down there." Frank shook his head. "Damn! Now I'm calling us that."

"Assuming we'd gotten our hands on whatever's at the compound, did you have plans for it?" Tony pressed. So long as they were talking about the drug, he decided to take a chance and let Frank in on the insights he'd shared with Charity.

Frank shrugged. "Nothing specific. Stockpile it. We didn't have any for years. It's like a well-padded bank account. An insurance policy. What would you do with it?"

Tony blew out a breath. "Since you inquired, I only want it for emergencies to stabilize those of us with genetic abnormalities. I'm done searching for the perfect version of us."

Frank half turned to face him, a neat trick in the cramped cockpit. "Did I hear you right? We finally have access to state-of-the-art labs and drugs, and you want to exit stage left?"

"You heard me correctly."

"Why?" Frank drew his dark brows into a concerned line. "I've worked with you for years. It's not like you to give up."

"I'm not giving up. I'm moving on. The search for perfection was the death knell for the breeding farms, and it damn near destroyed us once we set ourselves up in those compounds. Because we were so focused on the perfect iteration of us, we missed out on so many things we could've done with our existing ability."

"But we were planning to explore all that—once we were finished with V4," Frank protested.

"Listen to yourself." Tony fed a minor course correction into the chopper's computer. "V4 wouldn't have been the end. Or V5 or V6. We were chasing the impossible. I say it's time to learn to accept ourselves, flaws and all, and see how we can fit into normal human society."

Frank looked thunderstruck. Tony felt the other man's mind churning through probabilities, so he kept his mouth shut.

Frank set his jaw in a determined line. "Let's switch gears. Have you simulated data on the worst outcome from not recapturing the Cortexiphan?"

Tony blew out a tightly held breath. "Yeah. I did. If all the V4s take it, it might turn them into invincible killing machines. They could speed up their healing ability, so nothing shy of being decapitated would kill them. It might also enhance their innate talent to kill with their minds."

"You said *might* twice." Frank frowned. "What am I missing? I thought it was better than ninety percent odds the drug would do both those things—for the V4s, not for the rest of us."

"Their genome isn't much more stable than Charity's—"

"I know that," Frank cut in, "but it impacted their ability to reason. Tissue repair and focusing mind energy weren't affected."

"In truth, we hadn't fully explored the extent of the instability. More defects kept cropping up, the longer that version lived. They may have started out promising, but their systems eroded over time. It's almost as if they had a built-in self-destruct sequence."

"The drug should fix that," Frank persisted.

"We don't know," Tony said. "Not for sure, because we never had any Cortexiphan to work with."

"Are you suggesting if we leave things be, that the V4s will implode?"

Tony stared out the Plexiglas windscreen at the two choppers ahead of them as he considered an answer. "I just don't know," he said finally. "The V4s understood more about their flaws than any of us, but they wiped their information from the computers, which threw a clod in the churn."

"No shit." Frank made a rude snorting noise. "Bastards. The problem had to be worse than the rest of us suspected, or they wouldn't have gone to the trouble of scrubbing the computer's memory banks."

"My best guess is Milton will send the fighter jets in to finish things off at the Atchafalaya compound," Tony said. "The drug will blow up right along with everything else." He swiped his hands against each other. "Problem solved."

"Really?" Frank clanked his teeth together. "As the unaugmented humans would say… Bite me. That compound will be empty before we even get back to the naval base."

Embarrassment brought heat to Tony's face. "Of course," he mumbled. "We've got to come up with a way to track them. Maybe we should go back after all."

Frank tapped their fuel gauge. "Not possible. It would've been before, but we've put better than half an hour between us and them."

"Never mind. I'm not thinking. Finding them from the air through the thick canopy wouldn't work. They'll take boats and lose themselves in that horrendous swamp." Tony clicked his brain into hyper drive, running the odds, and smiled grimly. "Sixty-five point three percent says they don't remain in the swamp for longer than an hour or two. The other V4s will want the drug."

"Yeah." Frank grinned back. "I already figured that part out."

"What? You were testing me?"

"Nah. That conclusion occurred to both of us at about the same time. We'll be at the base in eighteen minutes. Do you suppose we'll head to Langley tonight?"

"Not unless Milton gives up on finding the Cortexiphan. Why?" Tony quirked a brow.

"Don't repeat this, but I miss my cozy lab. Even in the compound, I rarely went anywhere. Sometimes I was bored, but…" He let his words trail off.

"Funny, but Charity said almost exactly the same thing."

"It's difficult to believe one of the women would miss the compounds."

"I don't think it's the compounds so much," Tony said, thoughtfully, "but a life all of us got used to. We're augmented humans, not machines with human traits. It makes a difference."

Frank looked askance at him. "Next thing, you'll be talking about nest building and a homing instinct."

"We're scarcely pigeons, but we took a huge chance when we asked for amnesty. Even as our compound lay in rubble at our feet, with the rest of us holed up a mile away."

"We'd discussed it," Frank protested. "Ran the odds."

"It was still a big fat fucking bridge we stepped off. Into unknown territory." Tony inhaled sharply. "This conversation is a good illustration that, despite seven years of selective breeding plus whatever the farms did before we took over, there're still vast differences between us. Your cerebrum leads, and mine's balanced against my limbic system—the emotional part of my brain."

"Your point? Give the bird back. I want to land it." Frank set the helicopter into a descending arc, aiming for the base dead ahead.

"Back to Cortexiphan. We can't assume it'll have the same effect on the V4s as it would have on us. It's likely every single V4 who takes it will have a different reaction. It'll turn some of them into super-warriors, and drive others mad."

"Neither of those options is good."

"Agreed." Tony straightened in his seat and snapped his fingers. "I've got it."

"Got what?"

"I know how we can track the freaks and the drug. If we're quick enough, we can keep whoever's fleeing through the swamp from disseminating it."

"Spill it." Frank narrowed his eyes. "We need to refine whatever it is before we toss it in front of Milton."

"Why?"

"So he can't pick too many holes in it."

Tony smirked. "Wait until I'm done, then refine away. Humans are a stodgy lot, with limited imaginations. The closer to bulletproof this is, the better chance we have of it happening."

CHAPTER 9

harity hopped down from the chopper and declined the shuttle ride, preferring to jog back to her quarters from where the bird dropped them off on the tarmac. Her mind was full of Tony and what she would say to him—if she decided to say anything at all. She was still ambivalent about opening her closely guarded inner thoughts to anyone. If she kept her mouth shut, she could still cloak herself in pretending to not care. It was a hell of a lot safer. He probably sensed her confusion the previous night in her room, but she hadn't disclosed much then. Continuing to stonewall him wouldn't be all that hard.

Glory and Honor seem happy.

Maybe. But their relationships are new. Especially Honor's.

Her friends had left the flight line arm and arm with their men. Everyone else caught a ride, except for Frank and Tony. Their craft was a few minutes behind the other two. She waited until it settled, bouncing a little in the ground cushion, before turning toward her building half a mile distant. She considered waiting for Tony, but that might be awkward since Frank would be with him. Maybe the men had plans for the rest of the day.

Between their problems in the Atchafalaya, escorting the

downed pilot, and the next day's helicopter mission, a day and a half had passed. The midday sun felt hot and sticky. They were supposed to clean up, grab a nap, and meet in the building next to the mess hall at fifteen hundred.

Food and the next set of orders would be forthcoming.

A wry laugh forced its way out as she ran, and she pushed herself to move faster. She hadn't had any freedom in the compound, and she didn't have much more working for Milton. For some reason where she was now felt better, but that could be illusory.

Charity understood she was filling her mind with fluff to avoid making a decision. Even if she talked with Tony, it didn't necessarily mean anything. They might not be able to come to a meeting of the minds where they both agreed on parameters…

"Oh for fuck's sake," she sputtered. "This isn't a set of schematics, it's emotions."

Yeah, no wonder I'm so uncomfortable.

She glanced up to double check she was headed in the right direction. She'd been distracted, not paying attention, but part of her brain must've been engaged because she spied her building a hundred yards away.

Familiar energy flared nearby. Charity tensed and almost stopped moving, but forced her feet to maintain their rhythm. Tony was behind her and closing fast. Part of her was pleased, another part horrified. She wanted to control how and when they came together, and the choice was being snatched away. Uncomfortable flutters began in her stomach and sent shockwaves outward along her nerve trunks.

"How come you're by yourself?" he asked as he drew even with her. "I saw almost everyone but you get into the minibus."

She shrugged, but didn't slow her pace. "I wanted to stretch my legs. We were cooped up for hours between the helicopter this morning and yesterday's boat ride. Where's Frank?"

"On his way to his room, but probably behind us, since I ran hard to catch up with you."

"Was there something specific you needed?" She did slow then because they were almost at their building. Charity was hedging, but she hadn't fully made up her mind which horse she was going to ride.

"I was hoping for some time alone, so we could talk." He inserted his body between her and the door into their quarters and captured her gaze with his. Warmth and caring shone in the depths of his amber eyes. He grabbed her wrist. Not hard, but firmly enough she'd have to work to free herself.

Heat threaded a track between her legs, and the flutters got so bad her knees shook. If this kept up, the only talking they'd be doing would be about getting their clothes out of the way.

"Charity." He tilted her chin with a begrimed finger. "Are you willing to do that?"

"Do what? Talk?"

"Yes. We need to. Frank and I kicked an idea around right before we landed. If Milton buys it, things will get crazy again for at least another twenty-four hours."

"What kind of idea? Is that what you want to talk about?"

Tony shook his head. "I'll discuss it at fifteen hundred. I'm selfish enough to want this time for us."

Heat swooshed from her belly up her chest and over the top of her head. Words wouldn't come, so she just nodded at the door.

A slow, lazy smile lit his craggy face. "Your room or mine?"

Charity smiled back, suddenly shy. "That sounds suspiciously like a come-on line. Mine's closer."

He pulled the building door open for her, and she led the way to her room. Once they were inside, nervous energy burned a track through her body, and she flexed her fingers not knowing what to say or do next. Should she launch into a stammering explanation of the approach-avoidance feelings she had toward him? She dropped her rifle in a corner and removed her rucksack. Next came her shoulder harness, sidearm, and knives.

Tony divested himself of the same items before making his way to one of the room's two chairs and motioning her into it. "I'm jittery too," he said as he hooked the other chair with his boot and settled into it backward, crossing his arms across the backrest.

"*Jittery* doesn't quite do it," she squeaked. "I'm petrified. Good thing we removed all our weapons, huh?"

"I won't hurt you." He cleared his throat. "At least I'll try my damnedest not to."

She sensed truth beneath his words. "You might not mean to, but our programming runs pretty deep."

An odd expression crossed his face, and he leaned toward her. "We were never programmed to treat the women badly." His mouth twisted wryly. "We set up all those rules, so you wouldn't find out how powerful you are."

"Yeah. I know that part, but I still don't quite understand it. What were you afraid of?"

"Power's a funny thing. The reasons people hang onto it aren't rational." He shook his head. "I don't want to talk about the compounds. I want to talk about us. I already told you I care about you, and I sense you care about me, or you'd have told me to go fuck myself when I showed up at your door last night."

She studied her hands and realized she was twisting them together until the knuckles were white. Forcing them apart, she tested several beginnings in her mind, but nothing came out of her mouth.

"Tell me what you're thinking," he urged, his voice soft, gentle. "I could go into your mind, but I won't. This has to be on your terms."

"Thank you for that." She wrenched her gaze upward and looked at him. Even though she couldn't see her face, she was certain it reflected longing—and fear.

Tony stood and walked in front of her, his eyes never leaving her face. He opened his arms and waited. "We're both filthy from the field, but you felt so good in my arms last night, it's all I've been able to think about."

She quested outward with her mind, but Tony kept his

shuttered. He wasn't exerting subliminal suggestions to coerce her in any way, and it gave her courage. Feeling like she was moving in slow motion, she gathered her feet under her and stood.

"I take it that's a yes." He closed his arms around her.

Longing trumped fear, and she hugged him back, letting herself enjoy the feel of his body pressed against hers. She ran tentative fingertips across his shoulders and down his back over his Kevlar vest.

He cupped her neck with one hand and buried his face in her hair. Moving her head, he strung kisses down one side of her face. "I've never kissed anyone before." His voice was rough, thick with need. He threaded his fingers into her hair and gazed down at her.

Charity remembered throwing herself against Milton's body and plastering her lips over his—before he rebuked her roundly and told her to go away. Convinced he was a womanizer, she'd been trying to protect Honor from making a big mistake by hooking up with him...

Charity winced inwardly. No reason to share that little secret—it barely counted as a kiss—so she murmured, "I'm sure we'll figure it out and angled her head, seeking his mouth with her own. All her carefully choreographed words—the things she wanted to make certain were hammered out before they got involved—fell away when he brushed his lips over hers.

Tentative at first, the kiss grew in intensity. His lips became firm, demanding, as he sucked, nibbled, and licked her mouth. She opened to him and let him slide his tongue inside. Amazing things happened to her body at his touch. She played with his tongue and pretended she held his cock in her mouth. What would that feel like? How would he taste?

He ran his free hand down her back and covered her ass, drawing her hard against him. His erection butted into her stomach, and he thrust his hips against her. She heard the rasping pant of his breath before he kissed her as if she was everything, the entire universe. Caught up in the tide of his need mingled with her own, she kissed him back with a fervor she didn't realize she possessed. She'd been trying to prove a point when she threw herself at Milton —that normal humans were assholes. Except she'd been wrong about him. And maybe, just maybe, she'd been wrong to avoid Tony too.

Kissing him was as different from kissing Milton as a light breeze was from a storm that spun you around and wrung you out. She wanted the man in her arms. Wanted him to move his amazing lips from her mouth and explore her body with them. Wanted the cock pressing into her belly to be deep inside her. Her nipples hardened beneath her layers of clothing and sent sparks to her pussy. She shifted, so she could rub herself against his upper thigh. Sensation ratcheted through her, and her hips developed a mind of their own as they thrust against his leg. Her clit swelled with wanting. When he jammed his leg harder between hers, pushing it back and forth, she came, panting and gasping and clinging to him, her mouth still glued to his.

Tony held her until her spasms subsided. He tore his mouth from hers. "You're amazing." He traced her cheekbone with the hand that had been behind her neck.

"So are you," she murmured, feeling shy, but so aroused it scarcely mattered.

He let go and took a step away.

"Is that all?' Disappointment clutched at her belly. Emboldened, she closed a hand over the tented front of his field trousers. "You didn't come."

Color splotched his tanned face. "I almost did, and that would've been embarrassing. Men are supposed to be able to control themselves."

She tightened her hand around his erection. "Let me get your pants undone."

"I want you naked too, but we need to clean up." He flicked a finger against her Kevlar vest. "There are breasts under there somewhere."

"You think?" She wriggled her hips. Her clit was still swollen, and it sent heat all through her body when it brushed against her pants.

"Let go for now," He untangled her fingers from his cock. "I'm hanging on by a ragged edge as it is."

He started with her field jacket and unzipped it. Next came her bulletproof vest. The feel of his hands on her body as he removed her clothing was better than she'd imagined a man's hands could feel. He was gentle, but methodical. When she was down to her camouflage long-sleeved top and pants, she grabbed his wrists.

"What? Did I do something wrong?"

She pushed him backward until he ran up against one of the two beds. "Sit. We need our boots off."

She ran her hands down his thighs and calves, reveling in the feel of his body beneath her touch. No Kevlar there. He groaned as she kneaded his legs, and she let her gaze settle on his crotch. She wanted to see what he looked like. Needed to hold him, stroke him. What did a cock look like when it was coming? What would Tony's look like?

She felt the brush of him in her mind, heard his rapid intake of breath. "I want you too, sweetheart." His voice was husky with lust. "Need help with my boots?"

Charity giggled. "Guess I got sidetracked." She went to work on the laces holding his high-top boots in place, and he stripped off his jacket, vest, and the shirt beneath it. By the time she had both boots off, he was naked from the waist up. She'd been squatting next to him, and she rolled back on the balls of her feet—and forgot to breathe.

Broad shoulders, rich with slabs of muscle led to perfectly proportioned arms. Dark hair swirled around copper-colored nipples, and a hard, flat stomach disappeared beneath the waistband of his pants. Her throat tightened with desire, and her mouth went dry. With shaking fingers, she reached for the buttons holding his pants in place.

"We need to shower." He ground the words out. "The last thing I want is to let go of you for even a second—"

She set her butt on the floor and went to work on her own boots, begrudging them the moments it took to undo enough laces to slide them off.

"Shower?" he repeated and licked his lips suggestively.

"You just want to see me naked."

"Of course I do, but we stink. We have every right to after twelve hours in that swamp, today's mission, and no clean clothes."

"I can smell us too, even through the lust. It'll be a tight fit in the shower." Shooting an impish glance his way, she shot to her feet and turned her back to him as she stripped off her top and sports bra. She undid her pants and stopped long enough to slide them down her legs, pushing her sodden underwear after them. She wanted to see him naked. Bad. But she didn't let herself turn around.

In the bathroom, she flipped on the jets. Water pummeled the tile enclosure, and she waited a moment for hot water before ducking into the small shower. Her body felt electric, alive, and more aroused than she'd ever been. Coming from something besides her own hands was brand new, and she loved the extra tension thrumming through her. Her body felt like liquid sunshine, all golden and glowing. So much so, she was surprised to look at her arm and not see light streaming off her skin.

Tony pulled the curtain aside and stepped behind her into the hot water and steam. Prying the bar of soap out of her hands, he wrapped his arms around her from behind and soaped her breasts and belly. His erection pressed against her lower back, and he tweaked her nipples between his fingers. She leaned into him and felt her blood heat further from skin to skin contact.

Charity took the soap and set it on a ledge that ran around the inside of the shower. She turned in his arms and rubbed her soapy front against his chest and stomach, inhaling the scents of sweat, cordite, and aroused man. She opened her mouth to tell him how incredible he felt, but he covered her mouth with his. Where the last kiss had been tentative, this one took off immediately, starting where the first one left off. Their tongues tangled, and he sucked on her tongue and lips, bucking his hips against her.

Need pooled deep in her belly, and she reached between them to wrap a hand around his cock. It felt amazing in her hands, long and thick and perfect. He groaned into her mouth. His nipples turned into hot little buds of desire pressing against her chest. This time she was the one to break their kiss.

"Lift me up."

He blinked water out of his eyes and brushed shaggy hair away from his face. "Do you mean hold you? I already am."

Because words wouldn't come, she sent an image into his mind and watched his eyes widen with interest. Both of them were so naïve, it was astonishing they'd gotten this far.

Tony glanced around the shower enclosure and turned them so her back was against the wall and his beneath the spray. He splayed his hands under her thighs, lifting her easily, and she wrapped her legs around his waist. Keeping hold of his cock, she seated him at the entrance to her body and squirmed until he was inside an inch or so. "Push," she panted, after he didn't do anything.

"You're a virgin," he said. "Will I hurt you?"

"Maybe. I don't know." She pressed her nipples into his chest. "I don't care. Just do it. We've got to start somewhere."

Using a combination of gravity and thrusting, he worked his way deeper into her body. Need turned the world translucent, and the air developed iridescent motes. He entered her mind at the same time he stretched her body to bursting.

"Need the feedback," he gasped. "I'm so close, and I don't want to come before you do."

"I already came," she reminded him as she writhed around the unfamiliar object filling her until she almost couldn't breathe.

"You can come again. I feel your arousal." He withdrew a little and thrust into her.

She tightened her muscles around him and joined her mind to

his. The shock of feeling the heat of her around his cock amped her into a whole other dimension. She was drowning in sensation, drowning in the wonder of the man in her arms. She wove her arms around him and held on tight, raking her nails down his back.

"Look at me," he rasped. "I want you to watch me when I come, and I want to watch you."

Charity opened her eyes and found a new way to lose herself. Joined to his mind, his body, and his gaze, she felt every single wave of heat that pounded through each of them. Felt his cock swell, felt her clit burn with the need for release. And then they were there. She heard herself screaming and his grunting cries as his cock shuddered inside her.

For a long time, all she could do was cling to him while hot water pelted them. "Shouldn't waste water," she murmured, reached around him, and turned it off.

He reared his head back and looked at her. "That was the most unbelievable experience in my life, and you're worried about water?"

Laughter bubbled from deep in her belly. "Put me down. Let's dry off, and we can have a rematch in bed."

He didn't make any move to let go of her, just twitched his cock still buried deep in her body. "We've got something that works," he said. "I say we test it some more." Another twitch followed his words.

She tightened her body around him. If there'd been pain or a ruptured hymen, she'd missed it. He felt like he'd been born to be inside her, a wondrous plaything made just for her.

Small muscle movements cascaded into larger ones. Her next climax roared out of her, leaving her wrung out and shaken. Once he was certain she was done, she felt the ripples of his release.

"I could do this all day." His smile melted her insides into something sweet and foreign.

Charity grinned. "We're like a kid with a new toy. How much more time do you suppose we have?"

Tony lifted her off his cock and set her on the floor of the shower. "None, but it was worth it. I'll grab us something from the mess hall, and we can eat at the meeting."

"You won't have to stop by the mess hall. Milton promised us food."

"Oh yeah. I'd forgotten. Or maybe I didn't know that part."

If her mind had been a muddle before, it was ten times worse now. She opened her mouth to try to articulate her amazement—and her concerns, but he laid two fingers over her lips.

"What happened between us was perfect. Words will fall short."

"But—"

"He increased the pressure on her lips. "Time, darling. It'll take time for us to trust each other. More specifically for you to trust me."

"My genetics." She closed her teeth over her lower lip. "They're not stable."

"If that's the only thing you're worried about, we're golden. It's one thing Cortexiphan can fix for a V3, but I'm quite certain I took care of the problem when I was fighting to save your life."

"How certain?"

"Ninety three point four percent."

Charity ran her hands down his body, loving the feel of his skin. "Pretty good odds. I'll take them." She made a face. "Back into the stinky, nasty clothes. Wish I'd known how long we were going to be here."

Tony made a noncommittal gesture. "At least it'll force us back to Langley at some point."

"Either that or the local laundromat."

She giggled before it turned into a full-throated laugh. Tony joined her, and they laughed until tears rolled down her face. "Gotta get dressed," she choked out.

"Yeah, yeah. Wonder what they'd do if we didn't show up?"

"We probably don't want to find out." She blew a quick kiss his way and sorted through her clothes, hunting for underwear.

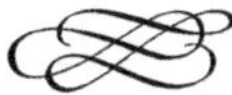

CHAPTER 10

Tony wiped another silly smile off his face and focused on the ham and cheese sandwich on the plate in front of him. He still couldn't believe he and Charity had made love. His cock swelled at the thought, wanting more. Thank Christ he was sitting down.

Frank elbowed him. *"I want to hear all about it,"* he sent in shielded telepathic speech.

"Bite me."

"It's not likely I'll ever get laid myself, so—"

Tony sent Frank a withering look designed to shut him up. He hadn't said a word; neither had Charity, but intuition ran deep in their makeup. Despite not saying anything, he was certain the joy streaming off them was visible, at least to freak eyes. Maybe to Milton and Roy and whoever else had taken the injections too, but normal humans were polite enough to extend at least the illusion of privacy when it came to bedroom matters.

He stole a glance at Charity, seated catty-corner across the table from him. Her dark hair curled around her face and hung down her back, half in and half out of her braids. They'd never gotten around to washing their hair, but at least they'd rinsed the worst of the dirt and crud out of it.

She worked on her sandwich like a starving woman, which wasn't surprising since dinner had been fast food, and breakfast was hours ago. Dear God, she was beautiful. Perfection itself. Her scent still clung to him. Vanilla and cinnamon and something distinctive to her. She glanced up and met his gaze, a small smile playing around her mouth. Clearly, she'd noticed his attention.

He longed for so many unfamiliar things, worlds he'd never truly believed existed before. Most of all, he wanted to take her away, just the two of them, so they could make love all they wanted and share each other's minds as well. He wanted to know every single part of her intimately, not just her phenomenal body. Beyond that, he wanted to take care of her, protect her. Nothing would ever harm her, not while he had something to say about it.

Frank elbowed him again. *"Milton's started talking. If you want to give our plan some airtime, look for an entrance."*

"First the good news." Milton took his place at the head of the room. "The Maine compound is history, and we secured the Cortexiphan."

"Excellent," Frank said. "We'll have some if and when we need it. It's a pain in the ass to synthesize."

Milton frowned. "Hold your comments until I'm done, or until I solicit questions."

Frank rolled his eyes but subsided into silence.

Milton nodded sharply. "The jets did another strafing run over the Atchafalaya location, followed by a chopper that dropped two men. The concrete bunkers took a direct hit, but there weren't any new dead bodies, so I assume whoever was left down there escaped into the swamp in one or more boats. Along with the Cortexiphan, which we also couldn't locate."

He stopped to take a breath. "Questions?"

"By new dead bodies," Honor said, "I assume you mean bodies

whose core temperature was congruent with having died just before the ground team swept the place."

Milton nodded.

Tony straightened in his chair. "Do you have a specific plan to go after those who fled?"

Milton frowned. "No, but from the tone of your question, I'm betting you do."

"Yes. It's not particularly dangerous, but it requires a fine hand because the clues will be subtle."

"Woot!" Charlie fist pumped the air. "Bring that baby on."

"Delicate operations are our specialty." David grinned. "It's where we live."

Milton shot an indulgent, paternal glance at his men. "You're both cute, now shut up."

"Yes, Uncle Miltie. Sir." David stared down his boss.

Milton, who seemed to be struggling not to laugh, jabbed his fingers in Tony's direction. "Let's hear it. Absent a viable plan, I'm taking us back to Langley."

Tony nodded. "We…" He gestured to encompass the women, Frank, and himself, "…leave a sort of phosphorescence in our wake. It doesn't last for much more than twenty-four hours, but it makes us easy to track with our enhanced vision. At least on land."

"How about on water?" Milton cut in.

"That makes things a little tougher," Frank said, "but Tony and I believe we should be able to pick something up. The water in that swamp is quite dense because of all the decaying vegetation. If they rowed their boats, and they'd damn near have to because of how shallow the water is on the other side of the compound, they'll shed cells along the way—"

"Those cells should float," Tony broke in. "If we're right about that, we'll be able to dial in our visual function and track them to land." He cleared his throat. "The other option, which is slightly less certain, is Frank and I took a good look at the waterways on a map and their proximity to roads. There are only half a dozen places where they could hook up with a car."

"Why a car and not a helicopter?" Milton asked. "I considered the road angle too, but if it were me, I'd take to the air."

"We don't have aircraft," Tony said.

"It's difficult to rent them," Frank added, "without proper identification and licenses. The freaks who stole the drug must've used chartered or stolen planes—"

"Stolen," Roy cut in.

"All right, stolen." Frank nodded. "Which means they did a lot of pre-planning to secure them. The men fleeing the Atchafalaya compound wouldn't have had enough advance notice to set something like that up. Aircraft would be hard to come by so far into the swamp on a good day. Impossible at the last minute."

"How come you never just bought aircraft to bypass all that?" Roy asked.

"We never had any sort of credit," Tony replied, "since we tried to maintain a low profile, stay off the grid. Buying even a cheap aircraft with cash would've appeared suspicious, let alone a multi-million dollar one. Regardless, I'd give it better than ninety percent the fleeing freaks called a car to pick them up."

Frank cleared his throat. "Back to the jets used in the original heist. Since you know they were stolen, did you ever get any leads on them?"

Milton scowled. "Negative. The crafts' tail numbers matched similar business class jets that had been wrecked. None of the info on the pilots panned out, either."

"Fascinating," Tony muttered and churned the data, hunting for what it meant. "We must've teamed up with a criminal element."

"Is that something new?" Milton asked.

"Definitely." Frank looked uneasy as he spoke, his brows held in a harsh line. "Flying under the radar used to be paramount. Apparently, things have changed."

Milton unhooked his sat phone from his belt and tapped its

display. Once someone answered he gave terse instructions to set up roadblocks in several key locations. After he set the phone down, he said, "Listen up, folks. Here's the plan. We'll break our two teams into four and cover the roadblocks from the air. If anything cuts loose, we'll storm that location."

"You'd rather do that, than have Tony and I pinpoint their egress from the swamp?" Frank asked.

Milton swept the room with his dark gaze. "Affirmative. Further questions or comments?"

"I still like my tracking plan better," Tony spoke up. "Less manpower. Better precision."

"Bad odds," Milton said. "Only two of you know how to do that. If something kills you in the swamp, and that's possible given our last go round there, the plan dies with you. There's not time to train the rest of us." He shifted his gaze to Honor. "Is this phosphorescent shedding gig something you and the women knew about?"

She shook her head and glanced Tony's way. Concern cut creases down her forehead. "One of these days," she muttered, "I'd love to have a complete list of all the things the men didn't bother to tell us."

"It's all in that data dump I stole from the compound computer," Glory said. "It's just a matter of finding time to sift through it."

"It'd be easier for us to tell you." Frank spread his hands in front of him and met her troubled expression head on.

"Later," Milton said tersely. "Right now, we have bigger fish to fry."

CHARITY FLEW WITH CHARLIE, Honor, and Hope. They'd separated into teams with four in each, except the last one that held Frank, Tony, and Milton. Honor was functioning as Charlie's copilot, which left Charity in the rear of the craft next to Hope.

The other woman yawned and stretched. "I'm sick of flying. Even the swamp was better than this."

Charity rotated her butt in her seat. The place between her legs was sore, but in a deliciously sensitive way. "I hated the swamp," she said. "Dark, creepy, smelly, overgrown."

Hope angled her face close and pulled off her headset. "Tell me about it."

"The swamp? You were there."

Hope elbowed her. "No. I want to hear about Tony. You fucked him, didn't you? What was it like?"

Well, what was it like?

"I'm still trying to sort that out. It's not like we had a whole lot of time." She pointed at Hope's discarded headset. "You ought to put that back on in case something crops up we need to know about."

"Eh. You've got yours on. It's good enough. If you answer me telepathically, no one else will hear." She narrowed her eyes, clearly fascinated, and leaned closer. "When we talked about you and Tony before, I wasn't at all sure you were going to follow through."

Charity bit back a grin. *"Neither was I. In truth, I still hadn't made up my mind when he caught up to me on my way back to my room."*

Hope sent an appraising glance skittering her way. "What tipped the scales?"

"He was kind, not pushy. Nothing like the Nameless Ones at the compound. It made it easier to see him for who he is."

Hope reached across the aisle and squeezed Charity's hand. "I'm happy for you."

Charity rolled her eyes. *"Don't plan the wedding quite yet, but things are off to a much more promising start than I'd anticipated."*

"I'd kill for a guy," Hope said, a wistful note in her voice. "Actually," she leaned closer still, "I like Charlie, but I'm pretty sure he has a girlfriend."

"I don't think so."

"Why not?"

Heat moved from her chest to her face, and she felt herself blush.

"When I hacked into the personnel database to check on Milton, I, um, checked the rest of the men too. At least the ones on Roy's team."

Interest flared in Hope's eyes. "What'd you find out about Charlie? Come on, hon. Spill it."

"He was married—years ago. Nothing since then. Lives alone at the Langley compound, and he also has a house at Cape Cod that's been in his family for ages." She crinkled her forehead in thought as she accessed stored memories. *"His parents are dead. He has two brothers, both younger. One's an M.D. in Boston. The other has bounced in and out of mental hospitals."*

"Too bad about the one brother. You're sure there's not a girlfriend?" Hope persisted.

"Of course I'm not sure. There could be. Why do you think he has one?"

"He's so good looking. It's hard to believe some lucky gal wouldn't have glommed onto him."

Charity's headset crackled, and she held up a hand. Hope made a grab for hers and settled it over her head.

"Showtime," Charlie said, excitement thrumming beneath the single world. "We've got a hit. Hang onto your seatbelts, gals, we're moving in."

"Jesus! He sounds so fucking cheerful I could strangle him," Hope mumbled.

"They live for this shit," Charity said. "It's why they're black ops CIA and not teaching at some university. Roy's a lawyer. He could be in a posh office pulling down hundreds of dollars an hour, but he's worked for the CIA ever since he passed the bar exam."

The bird banked sharply and lost elevation so fast Charity's heart rate accelerated. She gripped the sides of her seat hard enough to make her hands cramp from strain. "Good thing he warned us," she muttered and craned her neck to look out the windows. They'd been assigned to different sectors, so none of the other craft were in sight. She threw her power wide open, searching for the others and felt them closing.

"Charlie! What's happening?" she asked.

"Milton's bird spotted them. He's setting down on the highway next to the nearest roadblock. We're joining him."

A knot of anxiety lodged in Charity's throat, making it tough to swallow. No Nameless One she'd ever known would roll over and give up. They'd sense the helicopters and use mind power to shoot them out of the air. Before she could voice a warning, their chopper canted alarmingly.

"Shit!" Charlie shouted. "Focus your minds and keep them busy until I get us on the ground."

Honor dove into the back of the chopper. Her eyes were wild, and she held her jaw in a determined angle Charity recognized. The other woman's energy slammed into Charity's mind. Hope joined them.

"First thing to do is locate those bastards," Honor said.

"Got 'em," Hope crowed and rattled off coordinates.

"Charlie!" Honor cried. "Take us north by northwest at this speed and altitude for three point five minutes, hover, and we'll take care of them."

Charity joined hands with the other women. Their mind meld strengthened with physical contact. They gathered energy, balanced it, waiting. Too early and it might not be enough. Too late and they could get blasted out of the sky.

The craft rocked alarmingly as it took direct hits from freak mind power. Charity forced herself to take long, deep breaths to maximize her energy. So long as no one took out the rotor, they'd be fine.

"Now!" Hope screeched.

Electricity pummeled Charity until she felt as if she channeled lightning. Her muscles ached with the strain of controlling the flow. Every nerve sizzled, but she couldn't slack off. Not now. They'd come out with their guns blazing. It made them a much more visible target.

"More," Honor urged. "They're still kicking down there."

"There's not enough of us," Charity ground out.

"There has to be," Honor said. "No time to retreat or ask for help."

Unfamiliar energy pushed into their mind meld. Charlie. "I'll give you all I've got," he said, "but you'll have to channel it."

Charity seized his power, weaving it in with theirs. "As good as it's going to get," she said, straining to articulate the words. "Go. Now."

The air around her lit with incandescent light. She didn't understand the mechanism, but his energy potentiated theirs. Good information—if she lived through this and could tell anyone.

The bird stopped jolting from side to side. Moments later, they settled lower, skids kissing the ground.

"Crap! Fuck! Damn!" Charlie shouted.

Light blinded Charity just before the ground shook in an explosion. "What happened?" she cried, blinking away the afterimage and trying to clear her vision.

"Milton's chopper took a direct hit," Charlie said. "Christ, I hope they were able to punch out. It's so smoky I couldn't see a fucking thing."

A low, keening moan rose from Charity's chest, spreading until it was all she heard. "Tony," she moaned. "Tony was on that chopper."

"Milton was on it too." Honor's voice was raw, wounded. "I can't lose him. I can't."

"You have no idea what happened. Save your mourning for later." Charlie stood over them, his eyes on fire with something untamed. Charity hadn't heard him leave the cockpit, and his presence shocked her thoughts out of their downward spiral.

"Pull your heads out of your asses. There's a war going on out there, and they need us." He unsnapped shoulder halters and dragged them to their feet.

Charity's eyes burned with unshed tears. Fury rocked her,

leaving a hot, viscous trail down her spine. "Let's do this," she ground out. "I want to kill every last one of those fuckers. I'm sick of them and their power-mad aggression."

Charlie punched her arm. "That's the spirit. Let's give 'em a dose of their own medicine."

CHAPTER 11

Tony thrust against the blasts speeding toward them with everything he could muster. Even with Frank helping, their helicopter jittered as shock waves tossed it around.

"Listen up." Milton yelled into his microphone. "Latch the side door open. Make sure your parachutes are strapped on tight. If I say go, jump. Don't hesitate. Don't look back. And for fuck's sake watch the rotor blade because we'll be auto rotating."

"What about you?" Frank asked.

"Don't worry about me. I can take care of myself."

Tony exchanged glances with Frank and muttered, "I'll get this part." He lurched to his feet and secured the door in its open position. Wind roared into the cabin, deafening him. Hanging onto straps attached to the fuselage, he made his way back to his seat. After he half fell into it, he glanced at the shoulder harness and decided not to hook himself back in. Fumbling with the clasp could get in the way if he needed to move fast.

"I don't have a good feeling about this." Frank undid his harness.

"Which part?" Tony grimaced. "Jolting around in the air isn't a barrel of laughs, but jumping feels unnatural."

"Nothing is unnatural. We're machines."

"Yeah, well the human part is in ascendancy right about now. I'd feel better if we had a chance to practice."

"Stop whining and help me." Frank clenched his jaw tighter. Power spilled from him in waves.

Tony rode the crest of them, lacing his power with Frank's. An explosion bombarded his senses, and the cabin filled with smoke. The bird canted hard to one side, but Milton didn't say one word about leaving. Let alone getting the hell out right now.

Shit!

"Milton must be hit, or he'd be barking orders." Tony pulled himself toward the cockpit with the craft spinning wildly. "See if you can stabilize it," he screamed at Frank. "I'll get Milton."

Whatever Frank did helped, but not very much. Tony staggered into the cockpit and found a gaping hole in the windscreen, with Milton slumped against his harness. He was still alive, but unresponsive. No time to assess what damage he'd sustained. Tony unclipped Milton's shoulder harness. It was incredibly difficult in the rocking, rolling, wounded chopper, but he hoisted the other man over his shoulder and made for the open door.

Frank stood next to it, his expression grim. "I'll take him."

"I've got it," Tony said and stepped into nothingness to avoid further conversation. He had two jobs: hold onto Milton and pull the ripcord. He expected a sharp jerk when the chute opened, but it was so vicious, it nearly yanked the unconscious man out of his arms. Frank's chute opened off to one side. Their chopper plummeted downward spewing smoke and fire, so close he felt the heat from it as it passed. Tony girded himself for shock waves from the explosion when the helicopter hit the ground, and worked the air currents to get as far from the crash site as he could. Not easy with two hundred pounds of deadweight clasped against his body.

Meantime, he had another, more pressing problem. How hard would they impact? The chutes were designed for one man, not two. He did some rapid calculations, and didn't much care for the answers. Maybe they wouldn't even make the ground. They were prime targets drifting through smoke-filled air. It burned every time he inhaled, but it also made them harder to see.

"Aim for the lake to your right," Frank sent telepathically, sounding rattled.

Good advice, but could they get there? They were losing elevation at an alarming rate. He estimated approximately three hundred feet remained between them and the ground, and the lake was at least five hundred feet away. He pushed mental energy into the air, stunned when he was able to alter his descent rate. Maybe he could make this work after all. The water would soften their landing.

Milton thrashed in his arms.

"Stop it!" Tony yelled.

"What happened? How'd—"

"Later. I have to concentrate."

Tony felt movement as Milton twisted his head, surveying their surroundings. "When we're thirty feet above the lake, let go of me."

"I've gotten us this far—"

"And I'm still your CO. Follow my orders. Safer for both of us. Your chute will drag you up once you let go of me. Take that opportunity to pick your landing site. Once the water closes over you, swim in a straight line until you can't see the chute over you in the water anymore. Then surface."

"Any idea why they're not trying to shoot us out of the air?"

"If I had to guess," Milton replied, "one of the other teams nailed them first. Someone will have seen our bird go down. We need to get on the ground before everyone lays waste to the world hunting for me."

Tony counted down. "Fifty, forty, thirty. You sure, sir?"

"I'm sure, goddammit. Now."

Tony let go as gently as he could and watched Milton jackknife his body into a graceful dive that cut the water's surface cleanly.

Tony gained a few feet of altitude, but he didn't have the kind of time he'd expected before the chill water of the lake closed over his head. Instinct took over and he made for the surface, only to be enveloped by the wet parachute. After a brief struggle with the nylon, he recalled Milton's advice and dove far enough under to swim until he cleared the edge of the chute. He made sure to emit high frequency sound waves to discourage any alligators and snakes living in the lake. He'd just violated their territory and didn't want to pay for that particular sin. Once he surfaced, he made for the nearest shore, dragging the nylon material behind him.

Frank and Milton met him as he pulled his body from the water. Frank broke into a grin. "Baptism by fire, eh?"

"You could say that." Tony reached behind him, searching for the parachute's clips.

"I've got it," Milton said, and the sodden weight of Tony's chute dropped away. "Follow me. Smoke's so thick, maybe we can make it to cover, and then we can figure out what comes next. Normally, we'd conceal the chutes under rocks, but I don't want to take the time."

Tony followed Milton's lead, bending low and crab walking into thick vegetation dotting the lakeshore. He did a second quick scan for alligators and snakes, not finding any close enough to worry about. Milton waded through a swampy bramble thicket and stopped in a dense grove of willows. He leaned against a tree and rubbed his head.

"You should let one of us check you over," Frank said.

"Yes. You were unconscious when I dragged you out of the cockpit, and you've got a hell of a gash across your forehead," Tony added.

Milton scraped the back of one hand across his forehead and looked at the amount of blood. "I'll be fine." He shucked his rucksack. Once it was balanced on the ground between his knees, he pulled out a small kit and worked by feel until two-by-two bandages secured with a bandana covered the worst of the damage.

"You're fast," Frank observed.

"Yeah, this ain't my first rodeo." Milton rolled his eyes. "I figure I got bonked by a piece of the windscreen when it shattered."

"We should call the others," Tony said. "How do you want me to do that? Telepathy or communicator."

"Neither. Until we know more, we're not giving our position away."

"I did a scan for critters. Two of them, actually. Sorry, wasn't thinking."

Milton quirked a brow and then winced when it creased his wound. "Probably okay. Even I can pick up energy bouncing off damn near everything." He glanced around, a speculative expression on his face. "We'll work our way toward the roadblock where we sighted a carload of freaks."

"We'd be safer if we could set up a perma-scan for danger," Frank said.

"How noticeable would that be?" Milton put his pack back together and slid it over his shoulders.

"We could make it less conspicuous," Tony broke in, "if we traded off fully human for our energy."

"Say more," Milton demanded, muttering, "Damn, I wish I had my rifle."

"Take mine." Frank unslung the shoulder strap and handed it over. "You're probably a better shot anyway, and I'd rather use mental energy."

"What I had in mind," Tony continued, aiming his words at Milton, "was a burst from me, one from you, and then one from Frank. Using different frequencies."

"It's possible no one will be looking very hard, especially if our other teams are keeping them busy," Milton said. "Not sure I can manage different frequencies, though."

"We'll take care of that," Frank said. "We'll do something other than what you're doing."

"Maybe they'll assume we went down with the bird, but it seems unlikely, especially if they locate our chutes." Milton shrugged.

"Whatever they think or don't think can't be helped. We need to focus on things under our control, not conjecture."

"If any freaks were paying attention, they'll know we ejected." Frank sent a penetrating look Milton's way. "Ready?"

Milton shook his head sharply. "Not quite."

Tony sidled next to him. "I know I report to you, but give me a minute. Because you had the injections to make you like us, I can get your healthy cells lined up to fix the injured ones."

"Be quick about it," Milton growled.

"Open yourself, so I don't have to fight you to get in."

"Done." Milton nodded his understanding.

Placing his hands on either side of Milton's head, close, but not quite touching, Tony quested inward. He found what he was looking for and rearranged things with laser precision. "Good to go," he pronounced and dropped his hands.

Milton narrowed his eyes. "Headache's better. A lot better. Later, I want to know exactly what you did." He hoisted Frank's AK-47 and started moving as he unclipped the safety. "Follow me," he barked, sounding like himself again.

They made their way through knee-deep swamp water with submerged tufts of earth and large rocks. Since they couldn't see the obstacles, Tony focused a small beam of power after he caught his foot in tangled vines a second time. Gunfire rattled all around them. The air was still thick and smoky, almost as if the dank humidity held onto it. He coughed reflexively and dialed in a secondary mechanism to clear his lungs that wasn't as noisy.

Progress was painstakingly slow, and he allowed himself a moment to worry about Charity. Her team had still been in the air when he'd jumped out of the chopper. She should be on the ground now, and he wanted to be by her side protecting her. He was about to suggest they try for a more direct route when Frank's voice intruded.

"Behind us twenty degrees north."

Tony spun and sent energy spiraling after Frank's to see what they faced. *Fuck!* A veritable army was moving in their direction. If it weren't for the swamp, they'd be on them.

"Stay back," Milton ordered. "No reason for telepathy. They know we're here." He shouldered his rifle and delivered a volley of shots. Frank sent jolts of killing energy in the wake of the bullets.

"Shields," Tony screamed as he spun a buffer around him and Milton.

Light arced off the invisible barrier, but at least it held. Tony poured power into it and felt something wrap itself around his lower leg. "Goddamn it! A snake. Frank, take over the shields. I've got other problems."

Tony refocused his mind power on the snake, pushing gently into its consciousness. No time like now to test his theory about being able to communicate with it—assuming it was genetically modified. If he grabbed it or tried to kill it, the thing would sink its fangs into him before it died, in a reflexive attempt to protect itself.

"Friend," he suggested. *"I'm not a threat, but danger is close. Now would be a good time to leave."*

The coils tightened, and Tony girded himself to find out who'd strike first. If the snake heard him, there was no indication. No matter what he did at this point, the snake would win, since it was already in position. *"Friend."* He tried again because he was out of options. *"I don't want to hurt you."*

He glanced at Milton, still firing rounds, and at Frank, who was doing a damnably good job of keeping the shielding taut enough to deflect freak power and bullets. Maybe because he'd withdrawn his attention, the snake's hold loosened. A flash of darkness beneath the surface told him it took his advice about leaving seriously.

Tony blew out a tight breath. It was irrational, but he hated snakes. He scanned the water around them, not finding any others, before he wove his energy with Frank's. "How're we doing?"

"Not good. They're shielded too, so Milton can save his bullets, and they're fifty yards closer."

Tony did a quick calculation. "Ten minutes to make it to us, at their current rate of movement. I have an idea."

He sent waves of energy pulsing outward and found what he sought, pinging power off a gaggle of alligators five hundred yards away. Since things with the snake had turned in his favor, it seemed at least possible to co-opt the alligators into unlikely allies too.

"Let's hear the idea," Milton said, sourly. "I'm fresh out at the moment."

Tony sketched out how he'd dealt with the snake, and his plans for the gators, with a few mental images directed into Milton's mind.

"Brilliant!" Milton said. "Frank, can you hold the shields?"

"It's what I've been doing," the other man retorted, adding a laggardly, "Sir."

Milton snorted back a laugh. "If we get out of this, I'm signing you up for a course in military protocol." He turned to Tony. "How can I help?"

"Can you sense the alligators?" At Milton's nod, he went on, "Chivvy them like cowboys do to herds of things in those old movies. Move from side to side and behind them, herding them toward the freaks."

Power shot from Milton, and Tony made a chopping motion with one hand. "Gentle. You don't want to scare them away. Or worse, make them target us."

"Got it." Muscles in Milton's jaw rippled as he concentrated.

"While you're doing that, I'll feed them suggestions," Tony said and hoped to hell this would work. He didn't have to wait long for an answer. The swamp reptiles were far better suited to rapid travel than humans, and a cacophony of curses and screams rose above the din of battle sounds ringing around them.

"Excellent!" Milton gave a thumbs-up sign. "Let's take advantage of this and get the hell out of here." He shouldered his rifle. "I'm beginning to see why you two prefer to use your minds."

"It pains me to admit it." Tony cracked a grin. "But both have a place. While I coaxed the snake to leave my leg, I noticed a better route. It's not quite as direct, but we'll be able to move faster. I want to get to where I can see how the women are doing. And everyone else too."

"That group that's after us won't stop," Milton cautioned. "We slowed them down, but once those gators are dead, the freaks will be up our butts like no one's business."

"Agreed. We have to move fast." Frank punched Tony's shoulder. "Go."

Tony didn't bother to answer. He sprinted down the channel the snake had taken. It led to shallower water, but it was still so murky, he couldn't see through it. Milton and Frank ran behind him, making *sploshing* sounds as their boots sucked in and out of the muddy bottom. He felt a displacement in the air and stopped so precipitously Frank plowed into his back.

"What the fuck?" Frank demanded.

"Something's not right," Tony replied and swung his body from side to side, seeking what had alerted him. He cursed his days spent in laboratories and not as a foot soldier. Maybe if he'd—

"Smart, but not smart enough," a voice boomed. The murk parted, and a dozen freaks stepped out of it, surrounding them.

"Oh, I don't know about that. Another twenty yards would've been better," a second voice drawled. "Less distance to drag them."

Tony drew himself up, surprised. After a brief hesitation, he extended a hand toward one of the freaks. "John. Not the best of circumstances, but we always worked well together."

"Past tense does seem appropriate, given the circumstances." John's amber eyes, with their vertical slit pupils, gleamed against the low light in the swamp.

"You might want to consider working for us," Milton suggested. "After a trial period to test your loyalty. It's a better deal than what you have. Unlimited access to—"

"Shut the fuck up," another freak cut in.

"Yeah," someone else said. "If we'd wanted your stinking amnesty offer, we'd have shown up on your doorstep."

"You're not thinking," Frank said. "The compounds' days are numbered. I know how unstable the V4 configuration is, which means you have to go back to bedrock, or stick with V3, with all our defects."

"It's only a matter of time before the women stage a full scale rebellion," Tony broke in. "Then you'll be beset from two fronts. You don't have the ability or manpower to fight two wars. Three if you count the one against normal humans."

"Doesn't matter." John sneered. "We seem to have outsmarted you, despite our inferior makeup and numbers."

Milton glanced around the circle. "It's clear you don't plan to kill us, or we'd be dead."

"Smart man, but that could change if you don't do exactly as we say," John replied tersely. "We heard about the injections that grant some of our attributes to humans. You've obviously had them, so we'll study you. As for you two," he swung to face Frank and Tony, "we can't afford to lose any more geneticists. It's back to the lab for you. Under armed guard."

"What exactly do you want us to work on?" Tony aimed for a conversational tone. He wanted to keep the other man talking so he could probe the environment to see if anyone—or anything—was close enough to help.

"It doesn't matter," another freak answered, "since you won't have a say in which projects are assigned to you."

"We never did," Frank growled. "Coercion never yields good science."

"Just look at the breeding farms," Tony tossed in to keep the dialog flowing.

"What about them?" the freak who'd spoken last asked. "Those scientists couldn't wait to get their hands on human DNA."

"At first," Frank spoke slowly, "but not once things went south with V1 and V2. Lots of them bailed after that."

"Only because they were afraid we'd take matters into our own hands," John retorted. "Enough talk. We have a car nearby."

"What then?" Milton quirked a brow. "You won't get far. There are roadblocks at every exit point from this entire area."

A shadow crossed John's face, but left so fast Tony couldn't interpret it. So far, he hadn't found assistance anywhere close. Pinpricks pummeled his mind, staccato and insistent.

"Friend."

Tony scrubbed the heels of his hands down his face to hide his shock. The snake was back, or maybe they'd followed it toward its lair.

"Friend," he sent back, choosing his words carefully because the freaks would hear and nail him. *"Friends help each other."*

"We're scarcely your friends at this point," John scoffed. "Nor are we likely to help—" His words died in a guttural snarl as he grappled beneath the water's surface.

Expletives exploded all around Tony as the freaks cursed, wrestling with huge numbers of snakes boiling through the shallow water.

"Now would be a great time for that rifle," Tony gritted as waves of energy set to kill strength flowed from his outstretched hands. "Be careful. Don't hurt the snakes." Frank joined him. They took out half the freaks; Milton cut the others to ribbons with his rifle. They'd have died anyway from viper venom, but this was faster. Blood, bits of bone, and grisly chunks of flesh filled the air. Snakes rose from the water in a macabre parody of a ballet to snatch food as it fell.

"Thank you, friend," Tony sent, wondering which snake had finessed their rescue. He pushed splattered gore off his face.

Frank blinked blood out of his eyes; breath hissed through his teeth. "Shit! Never anticipated that one. I was sure they'd find a way to lock us in one of their labs forever." He stared at Tony. "What'd you do?"

"Nothing this time. The same genetically altered snake I made friends with when it was wrapped around my leg decided I needed help." He took in Frank's bemused expression. "Never mind. We can kick this one around later. None of us ever considered animal allies before." He directed his next words at Milton. "You okay, sir?"

"Better than okay. I wasn't exactly looking forward to becoming a test subject." Milton grimaced. "Never mind. We got a gift here. Let's get moving. Once we've put some distance between us and here, it should be safe to radio our location for rescue."

Tony plodded after Milton and Frank. After a quarter mile, watery swamp gave way to swampy land. Not that it was much easier going, but at least he could see problems before he ran into them. He thought about John and the others. Would most of his kin truly be so stupid as to sign their own death warrants?

Surely life among humans was preferable to no life at all.

CHAPTER 12

Charity, Hope, and Honor formed a line behind Charlie as they made their way to the roadblock. Charity clung to her anger, afraid if she let go, she'd break formation and race toward where she'd seen Tony's chopper go down. What if he was trapped? The fucking thing had gone up like a torch.

He has to have gotten out. He's too smart to let himself burn to a cinder. Unless he's unconscious.

Charity wrenched her mind from the unthinkable. Now was a time to focus, not lose it.

The other teams were already on the ground, along with several men wearing Kevlar vests sporting the CIA insignia across their backs. Half a dozen black SUVs were parked at odd angles, blocking both sides of the roadway.

Faith and Glory raced toward them, but Charlie's terse, "Later," stopped them cold.

Roy trotted over from where he'd been huddled with several men Charity had never seen before. "Here's the plan," he said, grimfaced. "I plotted a grid search for Milton, Frank, and Tony based on where and when their bird crashed. We'll remain in our three groups. I've uploaded the map to your wrist computers, also the sector you're assigned to search." He stopped to suck in a breath. "Charlie heads his team. I head mine minus David, who'll take the third group. The agents manning the roadblock haven't seen any freak activity, so it's a good bet they're all still in the Atchafalaya."

"Can we try telepathic communication?" Charity blurted.

"Negative." Roy shook his head. "It's a way for them to pinpoint us. Right now, they know we're here, but they have no idea how many of us there are. I recognize the feel of their probes, and I haven't felt them—not yet anyway."

"Could they have driven out of here in the other direction?" Glory asked.

Roy shook his head again. "All the roads dead end. These wetlands are too overgrown to force a four wheel drive vehicle through, plus you'd sink in most places. Check your coordinates and get moving. Ping me at fifteen minute intervals with your location. No other communication unless you're in a lethal force situation."

"Where's all the gunfire coming from?" One of Roy's team asked. "What the hell are they shooting at?"

"We're going to find out," Roy said. "From the sound of the weaponry, they're not our guns, which means the freaks are armed with more than their minds. My best guess is they're shooting alligators."

"If they're doing that," Hope said, "they might've drained their mental power and are letting it recharge."

Another weapons blast sounded in the distance, and Charity balled her hands into fists. If the men had made it out of the chopper by some miracle, the last thing they needed was to be turned into target practice.

Charlie herded his team off to one side. "You've got better imaging ability than I do. Look at the map—"

"I already uploaded it," Honor said in a dry, dead voice that reminded Charity of rustling leaves. "Into my brain."

"Honor." Charlie gripped her shoulder. "Look at me." When she tilted her head, he said, "Milton is the smartest, most resourceful man I know. He's still alive. You have to believe that, or you won't be worth shit in the field."

Honor clanked her teeth together. "Got it. Sir. I don't require a psychological pep talk, if it's all the same to you. Sir."

"I don't give a fuck what you want or don't want. You have to be at the top of your game out here. Hard. Driven. Focused. I need your best effort. Damn if I'm going to be in the position of telling Milton you walked into a trap and got your head blown off because you were in a funk about him."

"Why not give her the lecture?" Honor jerked her head in Charity's direction.

"Why would I need to?"

"Shut up!" Charity screamed. "I do not want my personal life turned into a fucking soap opera. Let's go. Sooner we get moving, the better we'll all feel."

Charlie opened his mouth, apparently thought twice about voicing his thoughts, and led them away from the road.

"After you," Glory called after Charlie and motioned to Faith and Hope."

The thick tree canopy shifted what was left of the day's light into a gloomy murk that felt like something out of a Grade B horror flick. Charity shivered. The day wasn't cold, but the swamp gave her the jitters. She hadn't asked about probing for snakes and alligators. Surely that would be all right. They needed some way to protect themselves. Splashing sounded up ahead and moments later, she was knee-deep in swamp water following Charlie's back.

She'd never walked a grid before, but its mathematical precision mirrored the way her mind worked. So many paces in one direction, followed by so many in another. Time consuming, but it ensured they wouldn't miss any clues. Despite their orders to shroud themselves with silence, she investigated the swampy waters for predators with a quick burst at irregular intervals.

Charlie turned and waited until the women were next to him.

He tapped keys on his wrist computer, reporting their position to Roy, then gestured them forward. They'd covered about a quarter of their assigned area, and Charity chafed at their orders. She wanted to stretch her mind to at least see if Tony's life force still thrummed somewhere in this godforsaken, overgrown jungle of a swamp.

"He'll be okay, hon," Glory spoke into her mind.

Charity's eyes filled with tears and she bit hard on her lower lip. Gunfire roared nearby.

Charlie froze, intent, waiting.

Silence hung heavy around them. Charity felt it pool in the pit of her stomach. This was stupid. They had the ability to assess who they faced. Why not use it? Minutes ticked by, but they felt like hours. She exchanged glances with the other four women.

Honor shook her head very slightly. *"It's hard, but we stay put,"* she sent in speech focused for Charity alone.

Finally, Charlie said, *"Move out."*

Charity's gut burned from acid that splashed bile into the back of her throat. What had happened during the precious moments they'd wasted huddled like a bunch of cowards, waiting for the weapon fire to die down?

Fury surrounded Honor like a nimbus. Charity felt the other woman try to rein it in, but without any success. She bit down on her lower lip until she tasted blood. Could she live like this? Always scared shitless something was going to happen to Tony? From the look on Honor's face, she was having the same internal struggle about her attachment to Milton.

It's not like there're a hell of a lot of options.

Of course there are. I can go back to being alone. At least then there's only me to worry about. For some reason, the thought made her feel worse.

To divert herself, she panned a burst of energy out, hunting for alligator and snakes, and stopped cold. *"Halt."*

Charlie spun, his eyes hard and every muscle tense. *"What?"* He breathed the word into her mind.

"Dead alligators. Bunches of them. And cottonmouths in a feeding frenzy. They've glommed onto something. Shit!"

Honor charged past them, heading right toward where Charity had sensed the disturbance.

"Goddammit! Get back here," Charlie snapped. His telepathic voice sounded thoroughly pissed, but Honor didn't even slow down. Swamp vegetation closed around her. Muttering a string of curses, Charlie charged after where she'd disappeared.

Charity couldn't stand not knowing any longer, so she scanned for Tony's energy. The first few seconds didn't yield anything, but then she found him. Breath whooshed from her lungs, and her legs felt weak.

Yes! He's alive. Thank fucking God, he's alive.

She wanted to push around Charlie, but fury pulsed from him, and he was moving almost as fast as she could have, so she left well enough alone. Another tense five minutes passed, following the *splash* of Honor's boots in the swamp ahead of them. Glory, Faith, and Hope trailed behind her.

Charity's muscles tightened into rocks as she split her attention between making certain she was headed toward Tony, searching for freak patrols, and hunting for denizens of the swamp out for a quick meal.

A muted cry from Honor changed everything. Charity couldn't interpret the sound. It might be joy she'd found Milton alive, or desolation because she'd stumbled across his body. To hell with protocol. She rammed her body around Charlie, muttering, "Sorry," and leapt over obstacles in her haste to reach Tony.

He was alive, but beyond that she had no idea what she'd find.

Thick bushes parted, and she ducked beneath hanging Spanish moss, swatting at renegade insects that wanted to eat her. Five more steps brought her into a small clearing. Honor was crushed against Milton's body, the expression on his face so raw with relief, Charity looked away. Frank snapped off a jaunty nod in her direction.

Tony rushed from behind a willow's trunk. He closed his arms around her, tight, desperate, and she clung right back. "Charity! Jesus. God. You're safe."

"How?" she demanded. "What—?"

"*Ssht!*" Milton's voice cracked like a bullwhip in her mind. He gestured Charlie to his side.

Charity straightened and moved away from Tony. Honor wasn't in Milton's embrace anymore. She stood next to him, tight-faced, swiping at tears. They left grubby tracks down her face, but her joy was palpable.

Glory, Faith, and Hope joined them. "*See.*" Glory patted Charity's arm. "*Told you he was all right.*"

Charity sent a heartfelt smile her friend's way. Friends like hers were hard to come by, and she was grateful for each of them.

A hand grappled for hers, and Charity squeezed back. Tony. She cast a sidelong glance his way, thrilled beyond reckoning he'd made it out of the chopper in one piece. He grinned rakishly and winked. She wanted to yell at him for taking such big risks and scaring the shit out of her. She wanted to hold him close and never let go. Most of all, she wanted to know everything, and chafed against their enforced silence. Warmth bathed her mind, laced with caring and a fierce protectiveness. Tony inclined his head and held her hand tighter.

"*There's an army of freaks in this swamp,*" Milton went on. "*So long as we have the opportunity, our mission is to kill every last one of those fuckers.*"

"*Cortexiphan?*" Charlie asked.

Milton shook his head. "*If they brought it into the swamp, and they'd damn near have to, we haven't seen any evidence of it. Unfortunately, there are a million places they could hide it here.*"

Charlie straightened and clicked keys on his wrist computer, probably reporting in to Roy that they'd found Milton. Once he was done, he looked up. "*What's next, boss?*"

Milton eyed Frank, Tony, and the women. "*Can you sense freaks nearby? I need numbers and position.*"

"I'll look," Frank said. *"Better if only one of us scans."*

Milton bent his head close to Charlie's ear. Charity listened in shamelessly, wanting to know what was going on.

"Raise Roy again," Milton instructed. "Have him redirect the teams and whoever's working the roadblocks. We need backup, as many men as he can spare and still keep the roadblocks viable. Tell him to standby until we radio coordinates."

Charlie gave a thumbs-up sign and bent over his wrist computer, no doubt feeding coded information into it.

Charity wondered why Milton didn't just communicate with Roy directly and figured it had something to do with the coded radio frequencies that changed regularly.

Frank sidled to Milton and motioned the rest of them close. *"Fifty of them,"* he send in shielded telepathic speech. *"In three groups. One north, one west, and one between them."*

"Which way are they headed?" Milton asked.

Charity winced. His telepathic speech wasn't shielded. Maybe he didn't know how to do that.

"The road," Frank replied. *"Where else?"* He rattled off heading coordinates.

Milton tapped the display on his wrist computer and studied the map. He pointed to a route that should put them on the road in position to head off the freaks and keep them from leaving. Apparently Milton was all too aware of his inability to mask his telepathic words and had switched to communicating via hand signals.

Frank bent close. Charity felt a slight jolt as he uploaded the map's information into her mind. Presumably, he did the same to everyone. Charlie clicked keys, letting Roy know where they needed backup.

Milton motioned them forward with a terse hand movement.

Charity fell into line, with Tony right behind her. The last thing she wanted was more fighting, but she pushed her anxiety and concern aside. Focus was essential, or they'd never leave the

Atchafalaya alive. She felt the other women behind her and sent up a silent plea they'd all come through unscathed.

~

Tony followed Charity, relieved beyond words to be reunited with her. From the way she'd hurtled into his arms, she'd been as worried about him as he was about her. A flame of tenderness warmed him. Maybe they could work through her ambivalence about him being a Nameless One after all. More than anything, he wanted to gather her close and move them both to safety, but that would have to wait.

He gave himself a brisk mental slap and refocused on the swamp. They were far from out of danger. Even though he'd managed to co-opt one cottonmouth and a few alligators into helping him, there were a gaggle of them who weren't in on the *friend* agreement. A nasty looking spider dropped from a tree onto his shoulder. Tony swept it off.

Patches of bramble-covered ground interspersed with standing pools. Good thing. They could move faster when the ground was visible. Milton set a surprisingly quick pace, and Tony wondered if he was deploying his augmented senses, or if he just had good instincts. Maybe a combination of the two.

He thought about John. The man hadn't exactly been a friend—mostly because they didn't have friends in the human sense of the word, but Tony respected him as a researcher. The hatred in the other man's eyes had been hot and real—a take home message that no matter how appealing life with normal humans might be, seven years of programming would be insurmountable for most of his kin.

Tony shifted his attention to the map program running in his head. They'd covered half the distance to their rendezvous point. When would Roy and the others show up? Probably not until they hit the coordinates since they were closing from different directions.

The trees didn't grow quite so close together, as they moved away from the densest part of the wetlands. He swept his gaze from side to side. Even though he wasn't fond of the thorny thickets and heavy timber, they provided cover. He felt progressively more exposed as they trotted forward.

Milton halted when they were half a mile from their target, and waited until they caught up to him. He shifted his rifle from his shoulder to his hands and gestured for the rest of them to do the same.

A question about amnesty rattled in the back of Tony's brain, but he kept quiet. The freak's words about their *stinking amnesty offer* rose to taunt him. He threaded his arm around Charity, who stood next to him. She leaned close, and he splayed a hand over her hip.

"Extreme caution," Milton whispered.

"We're close enough, we could scan for them and either shoot or use mental energy to kill," Tony sent in shielded speech.

"They must know we're here. They're probably making a run for their cars, or they'd have taken us on," Frank added.

Milton narrowed his eyes. *"Fan into a line. Open fire at will."*

Tony cradled the unfamiliar assault rifle and opened his mind as he searched for those like him. Energy signatures pinged back, defined and unmistakable. He moved into position in a horizontal line, where they moved forward a step at a time.

Frank walked on one side of him, Charity on the other. A jolt of Frank's energy made him turn toward the other man. Frank jerked his chin forward and made a spinning motion with one hand. Tony understood perfectly and entered Frank's consciousness. They melded their energy; once it hit maximum lethal force, they pushed it outward at terminal velocity. And then did it again. And again.

Cries reached them that gave Tony second thoughts.

Frank spoke urgently into his mind. *"They'd do the same to us. No mercy."*

Automatic weapon fire rattled around them as the others opened on targets they either sensed or saw through their scopes.

Charity used her rifle, her eyes on fire with hatred for the Nameless Ones she killed. An unpleasant truth hit home. She didn't struggle with his indecision about their kin—at least not the men. As far as Charity was concerned, they'd done her wrong, and killing wasn't good enough for them.

She wasn't alone. The other four women looked just as lit-up as Charity, slapping in fresh magazines with a vengeance.

No mercy, indeed.

Because he couldn't help himself, Tony ran probabilities and came up with less than twenty percent that he and Charity could find their way together. Things had improved since his original eighteen percent guesstimate, but not by very damned much.

"Focus!" Frank blasted him with that one word.

Shame filled Tony. He'd left his partner vulnerable, while he wallowed in *what-ifs* about Charity. Burying his last line of thought ten feet under, he turned his full attention to blending his energy with Frank's and taking down as many freaks as they could find and target.

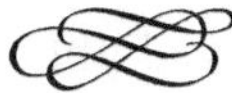

CHAPTER 13

The kick from the rifle irritated Charity's sore shoulder, but she was so high on adrenaline and bloodlust, she scarcely noticed it. The metal grew warm in her hands as she discarded clips and slammed new ones home. The only thing that stood out was that she was killing the bastards who'd made her life hell. The same shitheads who'd experimented on her already-shaky DNA. The screams of the dying were sweet, and she savored them.

"Why aren't they fighting back?" Honor hissed from next to Charity. "I've had shielding up, but nothing's hit it."

"I was wondering the same thing," Faith said, raising her voice to be heard over volleys of rifle fire.

Charity stopped firing long enough to consider the question. She sent her power in a broad swathe to see how many of the Nameless Ones were left. A feral smile split her face, making her chapped lips ache. Nine. Only nine left, which might explain why they weren't fighting back now, but it didn't explain it at the front end.

"Well?" Honor persisted just before she sent another volley of bullets in an arc.

"I don't know," Charity replied. "There aren't very many left. Maybe we should try to capture them and ask."

"I'll see what Milton thinks." Honor broke formation and loped behind the line toward him.

Charity worried if they kept firing there wouldn't be anyone left to question, so she edged next to Charlie. "Tell everyone to stop firing."

He turned to her, his eyes alight with pleasure that they were winning. "What? Why? We're almost there."

"If we kill all of them, there won't be anyone left to answer questions."

Before Charlie could answer, Milton's voice crackled through her communicator. "Hold your fire. Move out. Capture survivors. Use deadly force only if they threaten you."

Charlie sent an appraising glance in Charity's direction. "Why do I think you hatched this up with Honor?"

She caught his gaze and held it. "I'll never tell." Charity paused for a beat. "Don't you want to know why they never fired on us? Not even once."

"They sure did when it was just me, Frank, and Milton," Tony said as he came up beside them. "Not fire exactly, but they made it clear they planned to capture us."

"We can philosophize this fucker once we're out of here." Charlie pointed dead ahead. "You heard the man. Move out."

Charity felt Tony drape a protective arc around her and turned a crooked grin on him. "Thanks, Dad, but I was doing okay on my own."

"Fine." He shrugged and withdrew his energy. Before she could tell him she'd been joking, he turned and followed Frank, Milton, and the rest of the women.

What the hell?

The place where his power had touched her felt lonely, bereft. Sudden fear that had nothing to do with the Nameless Ones gripped her. Was he done with her so soon? It hadn't seemed that way when he'd hugged her against him in the thick timber to the east of them.

"Charity!" Charlie's tone was sharp. "Move out. Now."

She shook herself, tucked her rifle under one arm, and took off at a run after the others. Anger buffeted her, but it also drove Tony from her mind. She knew better than to get sidetracked—and by a Nameless One no less. She could dissect this later—once she was somewhere safe. Now wasn't the time to get lost in a funk over a man she'd fucked once.

By the time she got to a slender strip of asphalt, Roy and his team were already there, along with men she didn't know, presumably local CIA agents and other law enforcement called in to set up the roadblocks. Seven Nameless Ones were bent over cars getting handcuffed. What happened to the other two? Had they fought back?

Charity caught up with Roy. "When I scanned, I found nine still alive."

"Apparently there was a spot of dissention in their ranks." Roy flashed a wicked grin. "This group requested amnesty. The other two said they'd rather be dead." He snorted. "We didn't take them seriously until they tried to take David and two of the local agents out with mind energy."

Charity had stopped listening after she heard amnesty. There were actually other Nameless Ones who wanted to throw their lot in with them. "But that's marvelous news," she broke in.

"That they tried to kill us?" Roy frowned.

"No. That there are others who want amnesty."

"Well, they're going to have to prove themselves," Roy growled.

"You didn't make me do that." Charity drew herself up tall and stared him down. "Was it because I'm female, and you didn't think I could ever be a threat to anyone?"

An unattractive red began in Roy's neck and spread upward. "No. It was because by then I'd fallen in love with Glory, and I knew how decent you were. No one's ever accused the Nameless Ones of being decent."

"Frank and Tony are."

"We got lucky with them. Enough talk. I want to see if any of these bozos know where the Cortexiphan is."

Charity paced Roy to where the Nameless Ones stood in a row next to the cars. Milton was already questioning them, and she got there in time to hear a series of coordinates, where they could presumably find the drug.

Charity waited until Milton was done, and then she walked to the nearest Nameless One, put her hands on her hips, and asked, "Why didn't you fire on us?"

"Our orders were to take you alive."

"Why?" She heard truth in his words and strengthened her energy field to make certain to weed out any lies.

The man met her gaze. He looked determined, not defiant. "Our numbers are depleted. It takes time to grow more of us in the lab. We have the ability to use coercion to get others to do our bidding. It doesn't take long." He paused to suck in a breath and blow it out. "We saw you as replacements for our losses. You're all highly trained. It was too good an opportunity to pass up."

"How do we know you're not planning to try that once we get you back to the CIA?" Tony asked. He'd come up behind Charity, but her entire focus was on the man in front of her, so she hadn't noticed.

The man cocked his head to one side. "You don't. You obviously switched sides, so why can't we?"

"You can." Tony smiled with all the warmth of a cobra. "The question is will you?"

"Enough," Milton barked. "I need four volunteers to hit the Cortexiphan coordinates. We'll leave a car behind for you, but I want to get the rest of us headed back to the naval base and then to Langley.

"I'll go," Frank said.

"Me too," Tony squared his shoulders. He looked tired, and Charity's heart went out to him. It can't have been easy killing others like him.

"I'll go." She raised her hand.

"And me," Charlie said. "Someone with a driver's license has to be part of this posse."

Charity slugged him in the arm. "Hah! It's because you love us. The license is just your cover story."

He gave her back almost her exact look from earlier and said, "I'll never tell." The two of them burst out laughing.

"What's all that about?" Tony grunted, not sounding very happy.

"Private joke," Charity managed between giggles, but Tony's face darkened even further. She turned away. *Crap!* Not only was he a prima donna, he was moody on top of it. Falling for him had definitely been a mistake.

"See you soon!" Hope closed on Charity and gave her a quick hug. Faith did the same from her other side. Honor and Glory waved before trotting over to stand near Milton and Roy, who'd begun loading the Nameless Ones into cars.

Someone flipped a set of keys to Charlie, and he snatched them out of the air and tucked them into a jacket pocket. "Move out," he barked. "Watch for alligators and snakes. They haven't gone anywhere since our last trip through here."

"Want to hit the sites in order?" Frank asked.

"Yeah." Charlie nodded. "Let's go to the farthest one, and we'll work our way back."

Tony didn't like the fierce bite of jealousy that ripped through him when Charity and Charlie shared what she described as a *private joke*. She was his woman. His. She shouldn't have private *anythings* with other men.

What the hell is wrong with me? Half an hour ago I was horrified watching her kill Nameless Ones because she was so fucking thrilled about it.

"*Pull your head out of your ass and let's go,*" Frank said in shielded speech. "*I told you earlier. She's not worth it. None of them are. At least you got laid out of the deal.*"

"Shut up," Tony growled. "*Just shut up. When I want advice, I'll ask for it.*"

"*I'll keep that in mind.*" Knowing humor flashed behind Frank's amber eyes, and his supercilious attitude made Tony want to punch him.

Charlie moved between them, glancing from one to the other. "Whatever this is about," he said evenly. "Lose it right now. That's an order."

"Sir." Frank tipped his chin.

"Got it," Tony muttered.

"Good. Let's go." Charlie gestured to Charity. "Tight formation, single file."

Tony cleared his mind of everything but the task ahead. It took months to synthesize Cortexiphan. To have access to a ready supply would save boatloads of work. In the short time since they'd joined up with the CIA, he and Frank had barely had time to breathe, much less do any serious lab-based work. Charity walked ahead, between him and Charlie. Frank drew up the rear.

"*Sorry,*" Frank sent. "*Didn't mean to upset you. I'll back off.*"

"*That would be a good place to stop. I don't need to hear you say you were only trying to help.*"

"*But I was,*" Frank protested.

Tony swallowed bitter laughter. "*See how well I know you.*"

"Why are the two of you using shielded speech?" Charity asked. "What don't you want me to hear?"

Tony clenched his jaw into a tight line. He did *not* need flak from both sides. "Nothing," he said. "It was nothing."

"If it was nothing," she pressed, "you could've said it out loud."

"All of you stop this, right now," Charlie snapped. "Pay attention.

Scan for gators and snakes. I have no fucking idea what's up with you, but it stops here. I told you that back by the cars, and I'm telling you again."

Tony didn't say another word. Neither did Frank or Charity. Thank God. Frank was just being Frank, but he and Charity needed to talk. Carping at one another out here would just make things worse. Something drew his attention and he cried, "Stop! Gators to our right. Twenty yards."

"Fuck!" Charity spun toward the threat and muttered, "I hate this goddamned swamp."

Tony wasn't fond of it, either, but he got down to business and flanked Charity on one side, while Frank took the other. After a brief attempt to communicate with the gators that netted zip, he joined the others via a mind-meld and said, "Let's hit it. On my count of three…"

By the time Charlie made his way back to them, splashing, snapping, and guttural snarls suggested the alligators were either dead, dying, or heading for safer ground.

Frank blew out an annoyed sounding breath. "High frequency sound waves, people. Let's get this done so we can get out of here."

"Do you think that really works?" Charlie asked and sifted a hand through his shaggy, black hair.

"Yeah." Frank narrowed his eyes. "I do, or I wouldn't have bothered suggesting it."

Charity rolled her eyes. "I'm with Frank. Let's do whatever we have to, so we can get out of here. Swamps aren't my preferred environment."

"How's that shoulder?" Charlie asked.

"Eh. All that shooting I did earlier flared it up, but I'll live."

Charlie started walking again. "Can you do that high frequency gig and talk?" he called over one shoulder.

"Sure," Tony said. "What do you need?" He fell into place behind Charity.

"I'd like a quick primer on that drug we're after. What exactly will it do for you? And what could it do for humans if the side effects weren't so bad? For that fact, is there a way to alter the chemical structure to make it less toxic for us?"

Tony glanced back at Frank. "Do you want to answer that?"

"You can take a crack at it. I'll jump in if I need to."

"Thanks for the vote of confidence." Tony turned forward again. "Basically, the drug is long chains of linked polysaccharides—"

"Isn't that a fancy name for glucose?" Charlie cut in.

"Yes and no," Tony replied. "In this particular configuration, the chemical accesses the limbic portion of the brain, the place that processes emotion. But it employs molecular nanotechnology that actually links the limbic region to areas of the cortex that are particularly important for psi abilities such as precognition, telepathy, and focusing the brain's energy outward."

"Intriguing," Charlie said. "So intriguing, I'm wondering why it got scrapped."

"I wasn't living in your world, so I'm not totally sure," Frank broke in. "We always believed some of the test subjects went bat-shit nuts, and it was so irreparable the scientists backed off."

"Makes sense," Charlie said. "Next question. What impact do you suppose it would have on someone like me who took the injections to make me more like you?"

Tony ran probabilities before he answered. "Depending on what percentage of your genome is altered, I'd think it would be a direct ratio."

"So if I'm forty percent freak, I'd have a forty percent less chance of developing bad side effects. And a hundred percent chance of becoming even more invincible."

"It's not quite that simple—" Tony started, but Charity broke in.

"You'd be a fool to use that shit," she told Charlie. "No matter what the upside looks like, there are huge unknowns."

"You might be better off with more of whatever they injected you with," Frank suggested. "Do you have any idea exactly what it was?"

"Nope." Charlie shook his head. "But it was a bitch to take. Look sharp. We're fifty yards from the first target."

"We should stop right here," Charity said and halted so precipitously, Tony pitched into her back.

Charlie turned to stare at her. "Any particular reason?"

She looked askance at him. "All you have is the Nameless Ones' word about where they left the Cortexiphan. They could just as likely have left booby traps."

Tony started to protest. To say they'd never do that. The unspoken words left a bitter taste on his tongue. It would be very like something a freak would do, and he'd been worse than a fool not to mention it first.

"I'd considered that," Charlie said, "and discarded it because they're in custody. If we met with an unfortunate accident out here, they'd rot in a cell for the rest of their lives."

"That's how you think," Tony spoke slowly. "Not how we do. Their rationale would be that they're already out of the game, and however many of us they could drag down with them would even the score."

"I can see arguments on both sides," Frank said.

"Let's find out which one's true." Charlie started forward.

Tony pushed around Charity and Charlie. "Better let me do this," he said. "If there are sensors and bombs, they'd be keyed to your vibrations, not mine."

"You can do that?" Charlie asked. "Design things that detonate differentially?"

"Of course," Frank answered.

Tony wasn't paying attention to the conversation. He moved forward with his senses thrown wide open. Charity's energy pulsed behind him. This was the first of three locations. If all of them took this long, it'd be midnight before they got out of the swamp.

"Metal object just where they said it would be," Charity said softly near his ear.

He'd come to the same conclusion. His muscles tightened into hard balls of tension, but he kept his scans at full power. "Maybe you shouldn't be so close," he murmured.

"Maybe you shouldn't be," she countered. "Remember, my psi abilities trump yours."

A reluctant smile split his face. "I haven't forgotten."

"Halt!" Charlie said and hurried to Tony's side. He chucked a good-sized rock arcing into dense vegetation dead ahead. It made a metallic *clunk* before the swamp swallowed sound.

"Primitive." Frank snorted.

"I prefer to call it old-fashioned." Charlie grinned. "No booby traps here. Let's collect this batch and start back toward the other two."

While they waited for Charlie to load the small cylinder into his pack, Tony tapped Charity's arm. "Thanks for the warning we might've been walking into a trap."

She furled her brows. "At least one of us has to hold what those fuckers can do front and center."

Tony winced. He batted back defensiveness, hot words of protest that wanted out, since he was one of *those fuckers*, and there wasn't a damned thing he could do about it.

CHAPTER 14

Charity rode in the backseat of one of the CIA's black SUVs next to Tony. Frank sat up front with Charlie. Exhaustion tugged at her, and she slumped against the backrest. Until she was well and truly clear of the swamp, she didn't let herself think about how badly the combination of bottomless mud, alligators, and snakes rattled her.

Tony had been quiet since they got into the car. She tried to make eye contact, but he looked away. At least they'd recovered what appeared to be most of the Cortexiphan. Charlie said there was no way to be certain, just like there wasn't a way to make sure none of the freaks from the research compound had slipped between the cracks and escaped.

"Now that we have the drug, will you dose me with it?" she asked.

Tony did glance at her then and frowned. "Why would you ask? Are you feeling unstable?"

She shook her head. "No, but I never want to feel that way again. Guess I was looking for an insurance policy."

Frank turned in his seat to face her. "We'd only use it if you decompensated. No reason to so long as things are going well."

"What I want to know," Charlie cut in, "are the odds of making it viable for humans. I took that injection series, and they were a bitch. Headaches, muscle aches, gut cramps that lasted for months. Milton must be made of steel, since he just got the series and never blinked twice that I could see."

"I can't answer that." Frank faced forward again, addressing his words to Charlie. "Not until we get some uninterrupted lab time."

"Do you suppose that'll ever happen?" Tony spoke up.

"Not as long as the freaks keep us on the defensive," Charlie replied.

"How about the seven who are on their way back to Langley?" Charity asked.

"How about them, what?" Charlie countered.

"Well," she creased her forehead in thought, "once we find out what their special skills are, maybe you could use them on missions like this, and it would free up Frank and Tony."

"Not a chance, sister," Charlie said.

"Why not?" She felt confused.

"Don't you see?" Bitterness rode beneath Tony's words. "Even though we work side by side with them, normal humans still don't trust us, and they likely never will."

Charlie exhaled noisily. "We're selective about who we trust. Even with our rigorous background checks, freaks have infiltrated the CIA, so we're extra careful now."

"You accepted Frank and me," Tony said.

"Yeah, you gunned down some of your own right in front of us," Charlie pointed out. "When you said you'd sealed your exit route, we believed you."

"The group on their way back to Langley cited dissention among them," Charity said.

"Actually, Roy's the one mentioned it." Charlie corrected her. "We have to come up with a way to figure out if they told us the truth."

Charity bit hard on her lower lip. Things she wanted to say

almost choked her, but she took the time to sort through them. What emerged from her jumbled feelings was a question. "Do you want an alliance with us?"

The set of Charlie's shoulders stiffened, and he was quiet so long, she was afraid he wasn't going to answer. "It's not as easy as yes or no," he said at last. "We fought you for so long, all of us struggle with some residual trust issues. I suspect it's the same for you. Particularly for your men." He paused to take a breath. "All of us have people standing in line we don't trust. For you women, the Nameless Ones were at the head of the queue, but for the Nameless Ones, it was us—"

"Good summary," Frank cut in. "That sort of animosity and suspicion won't evaporate overnight,"

"I don't expect it to, but that doesn't make it any easier to swallow," Tony muttered.

"The thing I forget is you jettisoned everything familiar to throw your lot in with us," Charlie said. "That can't have been easy, but I don't think about that part when I'm worried about the integrity of the CIA."

"It hasn't been hard for us women," Charity said. "We have so much more than we had at the compounds, it's been a straightforward transition."

Color moved up Tony's neck and splotched his cheeks. He turned to her. "I'm sorry. I should've realized how bad things were for the women, but I didn't look very hard. We had so many problems, and..." He tried again. "I don't want to make excuses. Not for any of it. Some of the others might've wanted to make you suffer, but I wasn't one of them."

"I'm sorry too," Frank said. "We spent all our time in the lab, so we scarcely saw any of you females, except the ones like Faith who assisted with our experiments."

Charity's throat thickened. Nameless Ones were actually apologizing to her. She started to brush it off, tell them it was okay, but it wasn't. Not really, so she just said, "Thank you," and left out the part about it being too little and too late.

Tony looked away again. An arrow of disappointment jabbed her breastbone. Because she couldn't stand not knowing, she switched to shielded mind speech. The others would know they were talking, but wouldn't be able to make out the words.

"What's wrong? Did you decide what we did was a mistake?" She covered one of his hands with hers.

He did look at her then, and his amber eyes were full of pain and resignation. *"I don't know. We need to talk, but I don't want to do it here. I have to figure out what I'm feeling first."* He gently levered his hand out from beneath hers.

Her stomach tightened, and a slow ache began deep in her chest. To cover her pain, she shot back, *"We don't have feelings. We're machines."*

A corner of his mouth twisted downward. *"It would make things easier, but that doesn't appear to be the case. Not for you, either, or you wouldn't have asked those questions."*

She wanted to scream at him that he'd said he'd never hurt her. And follow it up with harsh words about how used and vulnerable and raw she felt. Charity forced a calm veneer. None of that would do any good, and she couldn't badger him for answers he didn't have. Answers that would send the tears behind her lids cascading down her cheeks. Instead, she moved closer to her door, shut her eyes, and tried to dial her mind down into sleep mode.

It didn't work. Thoughts churned beneath the surface that she didn't like much. Maybe they could skip the cozy little chat. When they got back to the naval base, she was heading straight to her room—alone. Unless they were leaving for Langley. Regardless, she'd had enough of men and false promises. Better to rebuild the walls that had always kept her safe. Her genome was stable, and she'd found a place she fit in at Langley.

The tension in her gut eased once she made her decision. It was for the best. She'd known from the gate that hooking up with a

Nameless One would be a mistake, and today slammed that point home. All in all, she was lucky she hadn't spent more time with Tony. The way things stood, she could walk away with minimal damage.

Who am I kidding?

Okay, more than minimal, but I can still walk away. And I'm going to.

~

TONY DOZED in fits and starts on the car ride back to the naval base, all too aware of Charity's wide-awake energy a foot away. She'd reached out to him, and he hadn't said anything to calm her fears. He could've crafted a soothing set of lies, but that wouldn't be fair—to either of them.

He cast a sidelong glance her way. Even though she wasn't asleep, the planes of her face were relaxed, and she looked so lovely he had to force himself to stay put. He wanted to gather her into his arms and rock her against his body, tell her everything would be fine, that they'd find a way.

His shoulders tensed when he remembered the look on her face as she'd gunned down freaks. How could she set aside the fact that he was one of the bastards who'd let the status quo survive? And for seven years, no less. The women's position actually eroded over the years after the rebellion. They hadn't fought back, and the men had gotten progressively more heavy-handed.

The SUV slowed as they approached the guard station at the entrance to the naval station. The young man at the gate waved them through, and Tony wrenched his thoughts back to practicalities. "What happens next?" he asked Charlie.

"You may have noticed it's well past dark. We'll grab some chow, shower, sleep, and hit the flight line at zero six hundred to return to Langley."

"What about everyone else?" Frank asked.

"They're already gone," Charlie replied. "They got back early enough, so it made sense, plus I'm sure the Navy brass weren't thrilled about finding a secure location for seven freaks."

"Where will you put them at Langley?" Charity narrowed her eyes and straightened in her seat.

"I have no idea," Charlie replied and pulled the SUV around to the building where their lodging was.

"Does Milton know they told us the truth about the Cortexiphan's location?" she persisted.

Charlie put the car in park and shut off the ignition. He turned to face Charity. "Yes, Milton knows. Why do you care what happens to those seven men?"

"Who said I did?"

Frank pushed his door open. He got out of the car and walked around to open the back, presumably to retrieve his field pack and weapons, minus the rifle he'd given to Milton.

Charity kept her gaze trained on Charlie and didn't make any move to exit the car.

Charlie shook his head. "You wouldn't have asked about them if you weren't concerned." She opened her mouth, but he held up a hand. "Enough. I'm bushed. You need rest too. Out of the car. I'll see you in the mess hall or on the flight line."

Charity frowned, but did as ordered and went to the open hatch to gather her belongings.

Tony got out too, anxious to talk with her, but still not settled on quite what to say. He could tell her she was so beautiful, looking at her almost broke his heart. He could say he longed for her, wanted them to have a shot at a life together. He'd have to follow that up with how deeply her glee at killing freaks cut into his soul, though. How would she take something like that?

He shouldered his field pack. Once it was balanced over a shoulder, he grabbed his rifle and other weapons, and followed her into the building. What should he do first? Go upstairs and drop his gear, and then see if she wanted to clean up and have dinner with him?

That might work.

He looked longingly down the hall toward her room and saw her step inside and shut the door. Would she be angry he hadn't followed her? Or relieved?

"For Christ's fucking sake, I'm overthinking the crap out of this," he muttered and trudged up the stairs to his own room. Half an hour later, his body was clean, but there wasn't anything he could do about his clothes. Anxiety soured his stomach and made his nerves jittery; both were parts of his human side he'd rarely dealt with.

Before he lost his courage entirely, he forced himself out of his room and down the stairs. He stood in front of her door as a minute ticked past, and then another. Feeling like the worst kind of fool, he decided against knocking and used telepathy instead.

"Charity. I'm right outside."

Yeah, state the obvious, why don't I?

Tony grimaced and realized he'd balled his hands into fists. When she didn't reply, he added, *"Would you like to have a late dinner with me?"*

He waited, but she still didn't answer. Finally, he sent energy forward to see if she was even in there, something he should've done right away. She was. He raised a fist and knocked on the door. When she failed to respond, he did it again and eyed the flimsy balsawood door. He could kick it down in a heartbeat, or defeat the lock with his mind.

The door opened in a rush and she stood in front of him, arms crossed beneath her breasts. Her field gear was scattered across the floor, and she was wrapped in the same blue terrycloth robe she'd worn the other night. Wet hair spilled across her shoulders and down her back. Her green eyes were deep pools of bitter acceptance, and something else he couldn't decipher. Anger, maybe.

"Get in here." She stepped back far enough to give him room. "Or do you want to have this discussion in the hallway?"

Tony moved far enough inside to push the door shut. Even

though it seemed like a bad idea, he held out his arms, but she shook her head, and he dropped them to his sides.

"I want to hold you, but this thing between us, it'll never work." Her eyes flooded with tears, and she turned away. "Leave. Just leave. There's nothing we need to say to each other."

Tony swallowed hard. "But there is." He kept his voice soft.

She twisted back toward him. Tears streamed down her cheeks, and her face contorted with silent sobs. "Do. Not. Be. Kind. It just makes this harder." She swiped at both cheeks, but her tears kept flowing. "I enjoyed what we did with each other, but if sex is our only common ground, there's no hope—" Her voice broke, and she turned away again.

He twined his hands into a knot so violently his knuckles whitened. "Please, just hear me out. If you still want me to leave when I'm done, I will." He sucked in a strained breath and blew it out. "This isn't any easier for me than it is for you."

"Which is why you should leave. Maybe we weren't designed to have partners. Even if we were, we ignored that side of ourselves when we set up the compounds. No one dated or had sex or anything else. All our babies came from test tubes."

"I know all that," he said, "but our basic genetic structure is human, so it's not as if we can't fall in love—"

She whirled, her eyes blazing with emotions he didn't have a name for. "Maybe I don't want any of that. It hurts too fucking much."

"You think I'm not hurting?" he demanded. "You're all I can think about. I'm just as confused and conflicted as you are, but I don't want to throw in the towel at the first sign of rough waters."

"Maybe I do." She squared her shoulders and stopped hugging herself long enough to place her hands on her hips. "I ran the odds out there in the field, and again driving back. They're definitely not in our favor."

"Depends what you feed into the equation as parameters," he countered. "I've done the same thing, and I'll grant you some scenarios don't give us much more than a twenty percent chance, but others are much higher."

Hope flared deep in her eyes, but she quashed it so fast he wasn't certain he'd seen it in the first place. "I don't care," she said. "They're just probability models. What counts is that I hurt…" She jabbed her breastbone with a finger. "…right here. And I don't like it. If caring about you comes with this kind of pain, I don't want it."

Something hot stabbed the base of his throat, and his muscles tightened into unpleasant knots. He tried to push his anger aside, but bitter words bubbled to the surface anyway. "How do you suppose I feel?" he demanded. "Watching your eyes light up as you mowed freaks down today was hard. You enjoyed killing Nameless Ones, and I couldn't figure out how you'd square loving one and killing others. I've battled with that ever since. It's what I wanted to talk with you about, but you're so determined we're done, you don't even want to try."

"That's right." She jutted her chin forward, but her lower lip trembled. "I don't. I asked you to leave half an hour ago. I'm asking you again. There's nothing we can say to one another that'll change a thing."

Fury bled out of him in a whoosh. "Sweetheart, there's lots for us to say, but I can't force you to see it. Maybe after we're back at Langley—"

She shook her head. "No. Not here. Not there, either. I'm sorry. I truly am. Maybe it's me. Maybe it's you, but this will never, ever work. Please." She pointed at the door.

Defeat tasted like ashes on his tongue. He used his mind to open the door and stumbled out into the hallway. It took him a few moments to let himself outside where he ran as hard as he could, circling the naval base so many times he lost count. Sweat slicked his body, and his heartbeat pounded loud against his ears.

Charity's words had been so final. He'd been certain they could find a way through if they believed in one another, but she didn't even want to try. He drew to a halt next to a building like all the rest on the base and slammed his fist into the stucco wall. Pain burst up his arm, but he did it again anyway. The unpleasant sensation cleared his head.

Feeling drained, empty of everything but a dull ache in his heart, he plodded back to his room. Morning would come soon enough. Maybe once they got back to Langley, he could lose himself in setting up a lab with Frank and getting some of his unfinished research projects back online.

CHAPTER 15

A knock rattled her door, and Charity looked up from her meal of a frozen dinner she'd tossed into the microwave. She'd been back for five days and kept to herself as much as she could, which meant showing up for her assigned classes and duties, but closeting herself in her room the rest of the time. The other women badgered the holy hell out of her, but Charity kept her mouth shut. What happened with Tony—and her decision—were her business. Mercifully she'd only seen him at mandatory meetings. He seemed just as motivated to stay out of her path as she was of his.

She still dreamed about him, longed for the feel of his arms around her and his lean, muscled body pressed against hers. Maybe that would lessen over time.

Yeah, I wish.

Whoever was out there knocked again. She sent energy skittering outward to see who wanted her and sat up straight, shock waves radiating through her.

Tony.

What could he possibly want? They'd already said everything there was to say. Why couldn't he leave well enough alone? If that weren't bad enough, her heart gave a funny little jump, and it was all she could do not to race to the door, fling it open, and throw herself into his arms.

Whoa! He's probably here on business.

Since their return, he and Frank had spent their time indoctrinating the new Nameless Ones and vetting them. Five of the seven panned out; the other two were on their way back to the compound of their choice. Charity didn't understand why they hadn't been imprisoned—permanently.

Milton tried to explain it was because they hadn't acted against the CIA or its operatives, but Charity wasn't buying it. In her book, the only good Nameless One was a man who couldn't ever hurt her.

"Charity. Please," rang deep in her mind.

She got to her feet, no longer interested in the food in front of her. It tasted like plastic anyway, and she'd only been eating for the calories. Gathering herself, she sent a jolt of energy to unlatch the door but didn't move closer to it.

Tony pushed her door open wide enough to walk through. He kicked it shut behind him, but then he just stood there gazing at her.

Charity gazed back, and what she saw stunned her. He looked terrible. Dark circles etched beneath his eyes. A fine network of lines she was certain hadn't been there before snaked outward from the corners of his eyes, meeting others that marched across his forehead. His cheeks held a gaunt, sunken look.

Compassion flooded her, and she took a step toward him, but stopped herself. "What's wrong?" she managed. "You look like hell. We don't get sick, so what happened?"

"What happened..." He sent a sad half smile her way. "...is you." He shifted from foot to foot and clasped his hands in front of him before dropping them to his sides. "I thought if I immersed myself in the lab, it would help, but I've been buried in that other project with Frank, and it's far from over. Now that we have five new recruits, they need training and programming to get up to speed on all the CIA policies and procedures. Weapons training. You know the drill because you've lived through it."

He raked his hands through dark hair, even shaggier than it had been the week before, and shook his head. "Hell, there's still an enormous amount of material neither Frank nor I are familiar with, and Milton stuck us with this teaching project. It's like the blind leading the blind."

Charity covered her lower lip with her teeth. Maybe that was it. He was here to ask for the women's help, but if that was the case, why not approach Glory? Or Honor? She straightened her spine. Likely this was a business visit after all.

"So…" She spread her hands in front of her. "You're here to see if I'd have time to help with the new guys. Me and the rest of the women, that is."

A sheepish expression spread over his face, and color added a golden tint to his tanned skin. "That's the official reason for my visit, yeah, but Jesus, Charity, I…" His throat worked as he swallowed hard, and he tried again. "I miss you. Holding you. Talking with you. I wasn't anywhere near done the other night in Louisiana, but you kicked me out of your room."

He took a step nearer to her and locked his amber gaze on her face. "Please. Charity. Give us a chance. We lost so much of our humanity at the compounds, I don't want to lose any more." He shook his head. "That didn't come out right. It's you I want. You woke something in me that I've never felt before, and it barely had a chance to begin to grow."

She couldn't bear to look at him, so she focused on her hands, still extended in front of her, and flexed her fingers. "Now that you've established connections with the limbic part of your brain, maybe some other woman could—"

He closed the distance between them dizzyingly fast. His energy pounded against her as he pushed her arms out of the way and crushed her against him. He kneaded her shoulders with strong fingers and murmured. "I don't want any other woman. I want you. Goddammit, Charity. I'm not eating. I'm not sleeping. Every time I close my eyes, all I see is your face and your incredible body."

Her arms crept around his broad back of their own accord, and she hugged him back. Still trying to hang onto rational thought, she said, "It's understandable you'd want my body again. It's the first time either of us had sex."

The grip he had on her back tightened almost to the point of pain. "That isn't it." His voice was thick with emotion. "You know that better than anyone. We have a mechanistic side. If you didn't mean something to me—something important—I'd have been able to walk away."

He leaned back enough to look at her. "You've kept your mind barred to me, but I've seen how you closeted yourself in this apartment. You're not interacting with anyone beyond bare minimums. Tell me truthfully you don't long for me the same way I ache for you, and I'll leave you alone. God knows how I'll manage it, but I'll respect your wishes."

She opened her mouth, dying inch by inch inside, but girding herself for the lie she'd have to utter, when he shook his head.

"Uh-uh. You have to leave your mind open to me, so I can sense what's behind your words."

"Okay." She reared her head back, but couldn't make herself let go of him. Jesus, he felt good in her arms. If she'd missed him before, it would be so much worse now that she'd had another taste of his body pressed against hers, his cock hard and hot against her belly, need spilling from him in waves.

Charity swallowed hard and left her mind open to him. "Do I miss you? Hell yes, I do. Do I want what we might have had? Of course. I'd be worse than a fool not to, but we have too many obstacles between us."

He cocked his head to one side. "I only see one."

"But it's huge. I hated Nameless Ones. Hated them. I still do. It cost me to volunteer to help with the new ones, but I'm willing to do it because I owe the CIA for rescuing me and training me and taking care of me. For offering me a life as a free woman."

"I'm a Nameless One, but you don't hate me." He dropped his hands to the curves of her rump and snugged her closer to his body. "Would it help if I agreed lots of us were assholes? They were. Outside of Frank, I kept to myself. Never had anything to do with the governmental structure of the compounds. In truth, I was grateful to have a lab where I could hide out, do what I'd been trained for, and not get involved with everything else."

A sour taste filled her mouth. "You were working on V4, which means you experimented on the unstable V3s like me."

He nodded. "Guilty as charged, but I was trying to help, not harm. Once I fully understood the futility of that line of experimental manipulation, I dug my heels in, took one of my only stands in seven years, and refused to be part of it. Our minds are linked, so you know I'm telling the truth. Plus, you could ask Frank. He'll corroborate what I just said."

"I don't have to ask Frank." Charity wrenched out of his embrace. "I can't think when you're this close, and I want you so much it scares me."

A different emotion—relief—pulsed through him, but he didn't try to hug her again. "Charity, we can't go back. None of us. I'm hoping you'll find a way to shut the door on our past. I'm trying to. I'm not proud of how the rebellion was handled or the seven years afterward. I want to start fresh—for everything. It's why I requested amnesty."

Caught between dread, indecision, and longing, she tried to hang onto all the reasons a relationship with Tony was a bad idea, and realized she'd let fears about her own stability rule her. What happened after her genome lurched into a downward spiral was still fresh in her mind, and she hadn't wanted to add additional stress anywhere in a life that felt precarious enough. Nameless Ones were her Achilles heel.

Could she see Tony for who he was beyond that label?

"I was telling the truth when I reassured you that you're all right now," Tony said softly, clearly still in her mind. His chiseled lips curved into a tender smile. "I should know. I'm the one who put you back together with my own kinetics."

A reluctant smile tugged at the corners of her mouth. "I'll always be grateful for what you did. You saved my life."

He sifted a hand through his hair. "I also fell in love with you. I can't turn that off. Please. Won't you reconsider?" He hurried on. "You don't have to give me your answer now."

Love? He just said he loves me.

Fluttery sensations stroked her insides. Tension bled out of her, chasing the dregs of her fears. Words tumbled out before she could modulate them. "I know I don't have to answer you, but you're all I've thought about too. I kept hoping if a little more time went by, it wouldn't hurt as much."

The crooked smile she loved lit his face. "Was it working?"

Charity shook her head. "Not very well."

He held out his arms, waiting, giving her all the space she needed.

Maybe it was his willingness to let her lead, but her reservations melted in the face of his openness, and she walked into his arms. He stroked her back and neck, murmuring endearments. "I can't say I'll never make mistakes, or that we won't have misunderstandings, but I'll try my damnedest to care for you."

"That's one of the stumbling blocks," she said, her words muffled against his chest. "Neither of us are used to letting anyone in." She twined her arms around him, reveling in the feel of slabs of corded muscle beneath her fingertips.

"We can learn together." He strung kisses down her cheek and caressed her back as if she were the most precious thing in the world. "I know it's late, sweetheart, and we're due at another briefing at zero six thirty, but I'd like to take you to bed."

All her pent up longing from the days she'd yearned for him and forced herself to think of other things roared to the fore. She dropped her hands to his ass and pulled his body hard against hers, desperate for the feel of him. His wonderful scent filled her nostrils. No cordite this time or sweat, just the clean evergreen scent of him mingled with spicy undertones that heated her blood.

"Bed would be wonderful," she managed around a tongue that felt thick and stupid.

"We didn't quite make it to the bed last time, but I'll give it my best effort. Enough talk. Besides, we don't need words." He angled his head and closed his mouth over hers, plumbing her with his tongue.

Her belly clenched with need, and every drop of moisture in her body fled south, pooling between her legs. Breasts crushed against him, her nipples pebbled into points of need. She shoved a hand between their bodies and curled it around his cock, delighted by the groan that escaped him as he pushed his flesh, rigid with wanting, into her hand. She hunted for the fastenings holding his pants in place, desperate to feel him skin to skin in her hand.

His lips hardened with desire as he kissed her. One hand cupped her neck, the other played down her back and slid beneath her sweat top. She started at his touch against her skin, and her breath hitched with longing.

He broke their kiss, breathing hard. "I want to see you naked. Have to." He exhaled in a rush. "Aw shit, Charity. I was afraid you'd built your wall so high, you'd never let me back inside. Thank God I was wrong." He hooked his fingers beneath the edges of her top and pulled it over her head. Her hair came loose from its sloppy bun and fell to her waist in sheaves of dark silkiness. When she glanced down, her nipples were peaked with wanting him.

He touched her breasts softly, almost reverently, tracing her hard, tingling nipples with a fingertip before he reached for her pants.

She batted his hands away. "I was afraid you didn't want me enough to try again." She pushed her tongue against her teeth, struggling for truth. "I was too weak to let my walls down. Too afraid to take a chance."

He reached down, swinging an arm beneath her knees, and lifted her into his arms. "You weren't the only one who was afraid. I almost didn't knock on your door. I stood out there so long, I convinced myself you had to know I was there and were ignoring me."

"I didn't. I was eating, not paying attention. She pressed closer into his embrace. "Are you taking me somewhere?"

"You bet." He winked broadly. "To your bed where I can study your body all I want. We were so rushed last time, I didn't get much of a chance."

"If all you want to do is study me, we hardly need the bed." She quirked an impish brow, teasing.

He growled something incomprehensible and carried her into the bedroom. Laying her tenderly on the bed, he slid her sweatpants down her hips, tossing them aside. He raked his gaze down her body then sat next to her and swirled a fingertip around the nubbin between her legs. It felt so good to have him touch her, she swallowed a scream and arched her back, pressing her pubes into his hand.

"Take your clothes off," she managed to grind out through a throat so thick with craving him, she was amazed any sound emerged.

"I'd have to stop touching you." He moved his hand in small, lazy circles around her clit. "God, you're gorgeous when you're hot. Your chest and face are rosy with lust, and your nipples are a work of art. He placed his other hand over a breast, pinching and twirling her nipple.

She bucked her hips against his hand, and he lowered his head, closing his mouth over her sensitive center. Sensation shot through her so fraught with heat, she thought she'd pass out. At first he moved his tongue around her nub, still keeping a hand on her breast. After a few swipes with his tongue, he settled in and suckled her. She did cry out then, the pleasure so hot and intense, she couldn't lock the sound in her throat. Orgasm pooled at the base of her belly and filled her with wave after wave of release as he sucked harder on her clit.

Once her spasms subsided, he let go and sat above her. "Now I'll take my clothes off." He pulled a stretchy green top over his head, and her breath danced in her throat like a caged animal.

Not that she'd forgotten what he looked like, but the sheer perfection of his chest, shoulders, arms, and stomach stole her breath. His nipples were tight buds of need akin to her own.

He kicked off running shoes and undid his trousers, pushing them down his legs and out of the way. His cock sprang from a mat of black hair, huge, thick, and long. She pushed to a sit and wrapped a hand around it, rubbing the dollop of semen glistening on its tip around the glans.

Tony gathered her into his arms and maneuvered them back onto the bed. He was breathing fast, and his cock jerked in her hands. "Easy," he murmured and pried her hands away from his erection. "I want to come inside you. I started to jack off so many times, but I haven't. Figured if I didn't, it'd cut down on images of you when I came."

He lay on his back and wrapped a hand around his erection. "Straddle me. That way I get to watch you when I come." His voice rasped with need, and he reached for her hips to help settle her over his cock.

Hot as if she hadn't just come, she lowered herself over him, delighted by how he filled her. He kept his hands on her hips, moving her but not too much.

"Touch yourself for me." He thrust into her, long and slow. "Show me how you pleasure yourself."

She cupped her breasts and fondled the nipples. They were already hot peaks of lust. Sensation spilled through her, and she pinched them. He kept a firm grip on her hips as he pushed into her, withdrew, and did it again. Another peak built deep in her vault.

Coming with him inside her felt different, more intense, sharper. She moved a hand between her legs and rubbed her clit in the little circles that would bring her off.

Tony slammed into her mind, and her pleasure rocketed off the charts. She felt the heat of her surrounding his shaft, felt him treading a ragged edge of control as he rode herd on his orgasm. At the same time, she felt him filling her, setting off nerve endings meant just for this.

"Feel me," he gasped. "Let's do this together."

Joined mind, body, and soul, she felt him judder hard inside her just as her own orgasm shook her, leaving her trembling and wrung out and desperate for more of the same.

Once their bodies stopped shuddering, he pulled her down on top of him and kissed her. He was still buried deep in her body, as hard as if he'd never come. Tony ripped his mouth from hers. "I love you, goddammit. You're everything I ever let myself hope for."

He twitched his cock inside her, rolled her onto her back, and started fucking her again. "I know you feel it too." He stared at her with his beautiful amber eyes. "Tell me. I need to hear you say it."

Her lips curved into a soft smile, and she wound her arms and legs around his body. "If wanting you so much it hurts counts, yes I love you. If seeing you in my heart and mind first thing in the morning and last thing at night counts, yes I love you. If barely being able to function because you're all I can think about counts, then yes, I love you."

He made a satisfied male sound just before he cradled her head between his hands, kissed her with a vengeance, and thrust into her until they both came again.

In the brief interlude between her last orgasm and when sleep claimed her, Charity murmured. "It's like you've branded me."

Tony laughed, and the sound warmed her. "Indeed I have. You're mine. My woman. And don't you ever forget it."

CHAPTER 16

"*W*here the fuck are you?" Frank screamed into Tony's mind, bringing him wide awake fast. It was still pitch black outside, four twenty-three a.m. to be precise, according to the computer side of his brain.

"*I'm not in my apartment,*" Tony said lamely, wanting to protect Charity, since Frank disapproved so strongly of him hooking up with her.

"*Tell me something I don't know.*" Hissing sounded through the telepathic link. "*Doesn't matter. I don't care who you're with, I need you. Right now.*"

"What's wrong?" Charity levered out from beneath the arm he'd thrown protectively across her body.

"*At least that explains where you are,*" Frank said acidly. "*I'm at Milton's. Get here as fast as you can.*"

"What happened?" Tony sat up and scrubbed the heels of his hands down his face.

"*Milton was too old for that injection series. I wondered about it when he first told us, but tabled my concerns since he seemed fine. Honor called me half an hour ago. Just get over here, goddammit. I'll fill you in then.*"

The mental link snapped off, severed as abruptly as it had materialized.

Crap!

Tony gave Charity a quick kiss and vaulted to his feet intent on throwing cold water on his face before he got back into his clothes.

Charity joined him in the bathroom. "I couldn't decipher that, but it must've been Frank. What's gone wrong? Is it one of the new guys?"

"No." Tony dropped the washrag he'd just scrubbed his face with over the sink. "It's Milton. He had a bad reaction to the injections he took."

"What injections?" She cupped water and doused her face and hands with it then dried off.

"The ones to make him more like us."

"Oh, those injections." Charity frowned. "But that was weeks ago. Why now?"

"I have no idea. Maybe once I get a look at him, it'll become clearer."

"I'm coming with you." Charity scooped clothing off the floor and dressed hurriedly.

"Not sure Frank will take that well," Tony said.

"Too fucking bad. Honor needs someone. I have no idea if she called the other women…" Charity's voice trailed off, and she shut her mouth with a clack.

"I'm fairly certain the only one she called was Frank."

"Mmph. Makes sense now that I think about it. She wouldn't have alerted Glory, not if Milton's trying to keep this hush-hush, which he appears to be."

"Why would you think that?" Tony pushed his feet into his shoes and snugged the laces.

"If there's something medically wrong with Milton, wouldn't you think his first stop would be the CIA's docs? There's some reason he doesn't want to involve them."

"Makes sense." Tony sent an approving glance her way. "I love your mental ability too. Not just your body."

"I'll keep it in mind, tiger." She yanked a fleece jacket emblazoned with the CIA logo off a hook. Once she had it in hand, she slid into it, zipping it to her chin. Next came a knitted cap and gloves. "Let's go." She unlatched the door with her mind and stood in the doorway waiting for him.

He trotted to her side and placed a hand on her shoulder. "One thing before we leave."

She furled her brows. "Do we have time for this?"

"Probably not, but I want you to promise me if you get cold feet again, you'll talk with me before you run the other way and exit stage left out of my life."

She nodded solemnly. "I can promise that, and I will. Can we go now?"

"Yup." He swatted her ass. "Let's hit it. I checked the map in my head. Milton's bungalow isn't far from here."

He vaulted down the stairs after Charity, admiring her easy, athletic lope that ate up three steps at a time. Once they were outside in a cold, drizzly predawn, they dialed in the afterburners and made it to Milton's front porch in a little over five minutes.

The door swung open before Tony could knock, and Frank grabbed his arm, dragging him inside. Charity pushed past the lintel before Frank could slam the door in her face. He glowered at her and opened his mouth, but she shook her head before he could tell her to leave.

"Stuff it." Charity squared her shoulders. "Where's Honor?"

"Right here. Jesus, I'm glad to see you." A white-faced Honor with eyes too big for her face moved into the room.

Charity ran to her friend, light on her feet, and swept her into a hug. Tony heard the buzz of them talking telepathically and glanced around a cozy, masculine space. The bookshelf-lined room held dark leather furniture arranged in inviting seating configurations. Oak tables with lamps made from polished wood were set at strategic intervals. A huge television screen took up most of one wall, and a computer desk with a large monitor of its own perched in one corner.

Tony eyed Frank. "Now might be a good time to tell me what happened and why Milton called you and not one of the CIA medics."

"Follow me upstairs," Frank said in terse tones. "We can work on him while we talk." He cut a diagonal across the room past the two women and mounted wooden risers leading to the next floor.

The entire second floor was one large room. It held the same comfortable ambience as the lower floor. A king-sized bed butted against one wall, with small tables on both sides of it. Mounted on the wall across from the bed was an enormous screen, divided into windows, each reflecting part of Langley's campus. The other side of the room held two armoires fashioned from dark, shiny wood. A desk took up the remaining corner with a computer and yet one more monitor. Across the room, a six feet tall, glass-fronted cabinet held a variety of swords and guns, mounted in an attractive display.

Milton lay across the bed propped on pillows with a blanket tossed over him. Frank made his way to the other man and ran a hand down the side of his head, scanning for vitals. Milton's eyes snapped open. "Try the drug, goddammit," he growled. "We're swimming in the crap now. May as well use it."

Tony joined them and nodded at Milton. "If you could start at the top, sir, it would help me figure things out."

"It's simple." Milton shook his head. "They said I was too old for the injections. I called bullshit, took what I needed from the lab, and gave myself the infusions. It was a bitch setting up the IVs, but I managed. I've done harder things in the field."

Tony narrowed his eyes. "What did they warn might happen if you took the injections?"

"Exactly what's happening now," Frank cut in. "Major organs are failing. It started on the flight back from Louisiana. I was in the cockpit and noticed he wasn't feeling well, but he brushed me off." Frank's nostrils flared in a mixture of annoyance and concern. "I figured he'd come into contact with some amoebic crap in the swamp. It never occurred to me the injections might've gone south."

"Prognosis?" Tony asked.

"Death," Milton cut in. "I want you to give me Cortexiphan. If I understand how that particular drug works, it'll fix me up."

"It could kill you," Frank protested.

"That's not all." Tony spoke over Frank. "It could drive you mad, which might be worse than being dead since psych meds won't correct the problem."

Milton struggled to a sitting position and pushed pillows behind him. He waved a hand, and the lighting in the room brightened. "Look at me." He stared at Tony. "My skin is gray. I'm losing muscle tone. Even my teeth are loosening. It's like I have a major vitamin deficiency mixed with rapid onset multiple sclerosis. I'm dying anyway. There's nothing to lose."

Tony clanked his teeth together and exchanged glances with Frank. At least now he understood why he was here. If they were going to dose Milton with an experimental drug, and the shit hit the fan, it would take both he and Frank to bail Milton out—if that were even possible.

He ran a quick probability model and winced. The odds weren't good—no matter what they did. And the number of unknowns was staggering. "The thing I want to know," he said and moved next to Milton, "is why the injections suddenly blew up in your face. How long ago did you get them?"

"Not that long," Milton admitted. "Just since the women came to live here. I figured I needed a boost to be an active part of the new training modules we were developing."

"I suspect that clonk on his head might've had something to do with this," Frank said. "Or jumping out of the bird. Or our trip through the swamp, or all of them mixed together because they created ongoing stressors that overtaxed Milton's immune system, so it couldn't control side effects from the injections."

"Makes sense." Tony ran his own scan and tried to keep a poker face, but it was tough not to wince at the damage. He cleared his throat. "What's happening to you is congruent with what your docs warned you about. The timeframe is likely about right too, even without all those things Frank listed."

Tony sucked in a tense breath and glanced at Frank. "What do you think?"

"Let's go outside and talk about it."

"No!" Milton thundered. "Any decisions about me will include me from start to finish."

The set of Frank's shoulders stiffened, and Tony knew he was furious. "Maybe it's better that way." Tony addressed his words to Milton. "If it were me, I'd want to hear all the possible bad shit too."

"There has to be an upside," Milton shot back. "Didn't you say there was something like a forty percent chance of side effects in humans? Since I got the injections, even if my body's in full rebellion, my odds should be better than that."

"It's forty-six point three percent," Frank mumbled. "And I think this is a bad idea. Maybe your doctors will have some sort of antidote for the injections."

"But then I'd have to tell them what I did," Milton countered. "Ill-advised career move."

"For Christ fucking sakes," Tony sputtered. "If you're dead, you won't have a career."

Honor and Charity topped the stairs and walked to the bed. Honor sat next to Milton and threaded her fingers with his. "What do you think?" She glanced from Frank to Tony, her green eyes raw with pain.

Frank shook his head. "I wish I knew more."

"Is he dying?" she demanded.

Tony nodded slowly, and she squinched her eyes shut, as if by not looking, she could erase his answer.

Frank cleared his throat. "I hate to bring this up, but don't you folks have rules against practicing medicine without a license? Neither Tony nor I are doctors. What would our liability look like if we dosed you with Cortexiphan, couldn't modulate its effects, and you lost your mind—or died?"

"No liability," Milton ground out. "If I wasn't too far gone, I'd tell anyone who wanted to know that I dosed myself with Cortexiphan, once I understood I was having a reaction to the injections I wasn't supposed to dip into."

Tony opened his mouth to argue that if Milton died, there'd be no one to exonerate him and Frank.

"Please." The single word tore from Honor before Tony could speak. "If there's any chance at all, you have to help him. Even if the probability models don't add up, you've got to try." Her face crumpled, and tears overflowed.

Charity stood behind her, patting her shoulder and looking so sad and resigned, Tony wanted to gather her up and send her back to her apartment. Maybe that wasn't a bad plan if they moved forward with the drug. People who got it went through a series of seizures that were agonizing to watch.

"Why don't you take Honor back to your place?" he suggested to Charity.

"No." Honor shook her head emphatically. "If— If the worst happens, I want to be with him. I'd never forgive myself if he died alone."

Milton turned tired dark eyes her way. "Maybe it's for the best, love. Tony wouldn't have recommended it if he didn't have a good reason."

She clasped his hand between hers. "I'm not leaving."

"What will we tell people about why we're not at the morning briefing?" Charity asked.

"Good question." Milton struggled to a sitting position and then to his feet. He plodded to his computer desk where he squinted at the screen and typed a few lines before making his way back to the bed. "Fucking hell. I feel about ninety years old. I cancelled it. Put it off until the next day." A shadow of his old, sardonic grin surfaced. "By then, I'll either be better—or dead."

"How can you joke about it?" Anguish ran beneath Honor's words.

He leveled his gaze at her. "If I didn't, I'd probably be crying just like you, and that's not my style."

"Where's the Cortexiphan and injection equipment?" Tony asked Frank.

"Why are you so sure I brought it with me?" Frank countered.

"Because I know you. It is here, right?" At Frank's nod, Tony went on. "I'm guessing the reason Milton's reacting to the injections is because they're making his cells vibrate at a frequency that doesn't mesh with his metabolism. A younger physiological makeup could tolerate it better."

"Say more about that," Milton growled. "I never bothered to pick anyone's brain when I decided I needed the injections."

Honor opened her mouth, but Charity tightened her hand on the other woman's shoulder and said something telepathically.

"All living matter vibrates at a particular frequency," Frank said, sounding as if he were teaching a college class. "Our cells vibrate at a higher frequency than yours. It's one of the reasons we have additional abilities. Whatever was in those injections simulated our physiology and encouraged it to invade your genome, making permanent changes—"

"—which apparently aren't sitting well with your body," Tony broke in.

"What will Cortexiphan do?" Honor demanded.

"If it doesn't hasten his death, it'll synchronize his cells, so they all work together," Tony replied. "Best case, it'll short-circuit the vibrational imbalance that's killing him."

"It'll likely enhance his psi abilities too, which is where the risk comes in," Frank said. Breath whistled from between his teeth. "Humans weren't meant to have psi ability. It's one of the reasons we were created in the first place." A stoic expression flitted across his face. "I could say a lot more, but there's no point. I'll go get my kit. It's downstairs."

As his footsteps clattered down the wooden steps, Honor placed a hand alongside Milton's cheek. "Are you sure, love?"

"Yes, I'm sure. Don't coo over me. It just makes this harder. Use that machine-precision brain of yours. Is there some other choice I've overlooked?"

Honor's throat worked as she swallowed. "No, but that doesn't mean I don't wish there were."

"If things get really bad," he cleared his throat, "I don't want these to be your last memories of me."

"That's why you want me to leave?" Her voice rose, taking on an incredulous note. When he nodded, she bit her lower lip. "We're not married, but I made a commitment to you with my heart and my soul. I'm not leaving just because you hit a rough spot."

"It's more than a rough spot." His voice was harsh and grating. "I fucked myself with my own hubris. If it means I pay the ultimate price, I'll go out kicking myself until they wrap me in a straightjacket."

"I'll never leave you. Don't waste your breath arguing."

He narrowed his eyes. "Yes, sweetheart. You will. If I end up a drooling idiot who doesn't know my own name, you will leave and make a life for yourself."

"It's not negotiable," Honor said, and her face twisted into a mask of pain.

Behind her, Charity caught and held Tony's gaze. *"What can I do?"* she asked in shielded mind speech.

"Not sure. We may need a third set of hands. We may need you to keep Honor from throwing herself into the fray."

"Got it."

The sound of Frank's footsteps attacking the stairs sounded like rifle blasts. Tony girded himself for an immersion into unknown territory. Not only had Cortexiphan never been more than a textbook concept, he didn't fully understand how it worked, or why it was toxic to some humans. Maybe it had to do with a particular biological marker they could test for—if they knew what it was.

He stole a glance at Milton and knew there wasn't time. The man was tough, but he was holding himself together by sheer force of will.

Frank pushed a few things out of the way on one of the tables dotting the room and began pulling things out of a black leather briefcase.

"Tell me how this will work," Milton said.

"We prepare an injection and introduce it into your spinal column right at the base of your brain," Frank replied as his hands flew over his supplies. "The drug will merge with your cerebrospinal fluid."

"Then what?" Milton persisted.

"Then we wait," Tony said. "We monitor your vitals and do what we have to do to keep you alive if you have a reaction we didn't anticipate." He turned to face Milton squarely. "You should know that neither Frank nor I have ever done this before. We never had the drug to work with."

"Maybe it'll turn out better than you expect." Milton struggled back to a sit. "Ready whenever you are."

"We'll need you lying on a flat surface, but on your side," Tony said. "Whenever you introduce anything into the cerebrospinal fluid, you have to remain horizontal until the body assimilates it."

"Even if you're flat and perfectly still, you'll probably seize anyway. That's where these come in." Frank waved a handful of leather restraints in the air.

Milton let go of Honor's hand. "Kiss me and then stay out of the way. I don't want to hurt you if I end up thrashing around."

"Come on, hon." Charity wrapped an arm around Honor's shoulders. "I'll be right here with you."

Honor's shoulders sagged, and she leaned into Charity, but didn't say anything.

Tony tossed all the pillows aside and positioned Milton on his side. "Okay." He gestured to Frank, who was filling a wicked looking syringe with an enormous needle. "We're as ready as we'll ever be."

CHAPTER 17

Tony stabilized Milton's head and watched as the needle slipped between his cervical vertebrae and on into the spinal column, shielded by bone, where fluid and nerves lived. Milton grunted once, but that was it. Damn, but the man must be made of steel. What Frank was doing had to hurt like a bitch.

"Can you hurry it up?" he asked Frank.

"No. It takes time for cerebrospinal fluid to accept additions. Actually, we probably should've removed an amount equivalent to what's in this injection, but I was worried about introducing two needles." He shrugged. "Each time I open the skin, there's the possibility of infection, particularly outside of an operating room with a sterile field."

The plunger in the syringe bottomed out, and Frank withdrew it very slowly. As soon as he was clear, Tony slapped an antiseptic sponge over the needle hole. Tension thrummed along his nerves, and his stomach churned sour bile that splashed the back of his throat.

Frank shoved his hands away and placed sterile bandage material over the injection site that he secured with tape. He pushed into Tony's mind, joining their energy. *"We have to be ready,"* he said simply. *"When things begin to happen, they'll go fast."*

"How do you know?"

"Educated guess."

"Talk out loud," Milton said. "That's an order. I want to know everything."

Frank grimaced. "Tony and I are linked. I want to be prepared."

"For?" Milton pressed.

"We don't know," Tony cut in. "We explained that before we started. Neither of us has any idea how you'll react."

"We do to some extent," Frank clarified, ignoring the pointed look Tony shot his way. "You'll seize. We just don't know what the endpoint will be."

"How long before something happens?" Honor asked in a thin, tortured voice that didn't sound anything like her.

Tony glanced at her and Charity, huddled a few feet from the bed. "Don't know that, either."

"How are you feeling?" Frank asked Milton.

"About the same. Weak. Like a mule kicked me in the balls."

"Headache?" Frank persisted.

"Not any worse than it was before."

Minutes ticked by. The sky outside the windows developed a pearlescent quality, signaling dawn.

"How much did you give him?" Tony asked Frank.

"Enough, if that's what you're worried about."

"Nothing seems to be happening," Milton said. "Can I sit up or at least have a pillow?"

"No." Frank bit off the word and chose not to utter an entire string Tony saw in his mind. Words that reminded Milton he'd asked for this.

Tony caught Frank's gaze in a silent question, and the other man shrugged. They were in uncharted waters, and they couldn't turn the boat around. Not now.

A tremor rippled down Milton's tall, muscled frame.

"Here it comes." Frank used shielded mind speech.

Tony moved closer to the bed, relieved this would finally play itself out, but apprehensive as hell about the genie they'd let out of the bottle.

"Goddammit!" Milton shrieked just before his body bowed then jerked.

Frank turned him onto his back and grabbed his ankles. Tony held his shoulders and forced a strip of hard leather between his teeth.

Milton's body shuddered and jerked as a puppet might have danced suspended from broken strings.

"What can I do?" Charity had moved next to Tony without him realizing it.

"Join your energy to ours," Tony ground out. "We're holding him. Barely."

"I'll help too." Honor stood next to Frank and grasped his arm to strengthen her mental link.

Encouraged by the additional power, Tony freed up enough energy to scan Milton's body and figure out exactly what the drug was doing to create such a strong reaction. What he found pleased him. At a cellular level, Cortexiphan molecules were bonding and shifting things. He saw the damage from the injections, which had been cumulative, start to repair itself. Likely the infusions began to create harm immediately, but it had to reach critical mass before Milton suspected anything was amiss.

"It looks like he's getting better," Charity ventured.

"Not that simple," Frank ground out. "Yeah, it's fixing what was wrong, but it might be creating other problems."

"Are you always this optimistic?" Honor's tone oozed sarcasm.

"I'm realistic," he shot back. "No more talk unless it's necessary. Focus on stabilizing his cortical areas in the temporal lobe that control seizures. We've got to get him past them, or nothing else will matter."

Milton's body thrashed and bucked. Tony wondered about the

restraints Frank had, but between the four of them in a mind meld, and him and Frank holding Milton's arms and legs, they didn't seem needed.

"How long can he survive like this?" Honor asked.

"Focus on the epicenter in his brain," Frank said, sounding rattled.

Tony spared a glance at daylight spilling through the window and guessed at least an hour had passed since Milton began to seize. He reached for the portion of Milton's temporal lobe that controlled seizures and probed.

Not good. Cells spun crazily, dancing to a tune only they could hear. "Stay with me on this," he told Frank.

"What are you going to do?"

"Excise the worst of the cells causing the seizures. I'll need one hand free, so you'll have to fill in for me holding him down."

"You can't fry his brain cells," Honor gasped. "It'll kill him."

"It's a calculated risk, but I don't think it's a lethal one," Tony said. "Besides, he'll die anyway if we can't stop the seizures. What I'll be doing is invasive and delicate. I have to concentrate. No more talk until I'm done."

A muted whimper escaped Honor, and Charity whispered, "Be strong."

Tony pushed into Milton's brain with laser precision and burned a small circle of tissue. He waited, barely breathing, and let a hand hover over the side of Milton's head, probing for exactly the right location. Once he had it, he thrust energy forward. It flashed, did battle with Milton's physiology, but entered his brain after Tony pushed extra kinetics after it. Once he had a firm bond, he sent his own cells into Milton's temporal lobe to heal the damaged spot. The channel he'd opened was fragile, so he had to be careful. Time slipped by as he worked, intent on repairing Milton's ravaged neurons.

"It's working," Charity said softly. "Son of a bitch. He stopped seizing."

Tony had been so intent on what he was doing, he hadn't noticed.

Frank's energy joined his, and the other man strengthened the layers of cells Tony had fused into Milton's brain. Between the two of them, the work went faster. Tony met Frank's gaze, nodded, and they both withdrew, taking care not to damage anything.

Sweat slicked Tony's sides, and he was breathing hard. At least they'd made it past the first hurdle. He hadn't actually believed they would.

"What now?" Charity asked.

"He'll remain unconscious for a while," Frank said.

"How long?" Honor narrowed her eyes, clearly intuiting there were critical things Frank hadn't said.

"As little as an hour, or as long as forever," Frank finally answered. "I just don't know."

"Can we do anything to help him or hurry things along?" Charity asked.

"We could," Tony said, "but it's better if he comes to on his own. We've already mucked around in his brain more than is probably good for him."

The strident chime of Milton's cell phone filled the air; everyone turned to stare at it. "What should we do?" Honor asked, eying the black plastic as if it were a snake.

"Ignore it for now," Frank said. "They'll come looking for him, but probably not right away. Maybe by then, he'll have come around."

CHARITY PULLED a chair next to where Honor sat on the bed by Milton. She'd started to place a pillow under his head, but Frank told her not to. Best case scenario, if Milton did regain consciousness, he'd have a mother of a headache, which would only be worse if he didn't remain absolutely flat.

An hour withered away, followed by part of another. Milton's phone hadn't rung again, which seemed impossible given the number of calls he usually got.

Frank and Tony huddled off to one side of the room deep in shielded conversation. Part of her wanted to know what they were saying, but another didn't. She felt proud of both men. They'd swallowed deep reservations and done everything they could to save Milton's life. Just like they did for her after she collapsed.

Honor stroked one of Milton's hands and glanced at Charity. "His brainwave pattern is improving."

Charity wondered if it was wishful thinking on Honor's part, but since she hadn't checked lately, she sent a flicker of energy outward and scanned Milton's mind. Because she wasn't certain, she did it again and smiled.

"I'm right, aren't I?" Honor asked. "I've been inside his head the whole time, so it's hard for me to tell."

"Yes, hon." Charity patted her arm. "You're right. The deep waves —theta and delta—are giving way to alpha and beta."

Frank shot to his feet and settled next to Milton. He placed a hand on either side of his head, hovering a few millimeters away, and a worried sound, somewhere between a sigh and a grunt, escaped him. "Soon. We'll have answers soon."

"I want to assess what's happening." Tony pushed between Frank and Milton and repeated Frank's actions.

"All he has to do is regain consciousness, right?" Honor glanced from Frank to Tony. "Once he does that, everything will be all right."

Tony narrowed his eyes. "We'll be past the second challenge once he comes around," he clarified.

"How many are there?" Honor's voice held a shrill, desperate note.

"The first was introducing the drug into him," Frank answered. "And nursemaiding him past the seizures."

"The second will be having him regain consciousness," Tony

broke in. "And the last is whether he'll gradually sink into psychosis."

"How long before we know about that one?" Charity asked.

"Pretty damned fast," Tony replied. "Either he'll be himself when he wakes up. Or not."

Milton moved his hand beneath Honor's, turned it, and clasped hers. His eyes flickered open and moved from one of them to another. "Why're you all looking at me like I came back from the dead?" His voice was weak, but it held traces of the sarcastic humor that was part and parcel of Milton.

"Maybe because you did," Frank answered dryly.

"When can I sit up? I'm thirsty."

"No sitting for another hour or two," Frank cautioned.

"Can I get him some water?" Honor asked.

"Ice chips would be better," Tony said.

"I'm on it." Charity sprang to her feet and clattered down the stairs. The hum of conversation from upstairs faded as she found a bowl and told the icemaker to deliver crushed ice.

Maybe, just maybe, they'd tossed the dice and won. Milton didn't seem much the worse for wear. What would the Cortexiphan do for him? Had it made him one hundred percent freak, just like her?

She shook her head and smiled wryly as she made her way back upstairs. Time would yield answers to those questions, but it was a sure bet that if the drug gave Milton even more superhuman qualities, Roy and his men would be quick to sign up. Charlie too.

She handed the bowl to Honor, who fed slivers of ice to Milton, one at a time.

"Is the worst over?" Charity asked Tony. When he nodded, she said, "We should go. If we show up at the places we're supposed to be, maybe we can buy Milton some time before anyone bangs on his door because they're worried about him."

Tony exchanged a pointed glance with Frank, who started packing things into his briefcase. "Good idea." He bent over Milton. "You're a tough old bastard. Once you're up to it, you owe Frank and me some lab time. We want to know exactly what the Cortexiphan did for you."

"You got it." Milton grinned, looking much more like himself.

"I'll stay here," Honor said. "If anyone asks, Milton came down with the flu, and I'm taking care of him."

"See you in half an hour in the small meeting room." Frank punched Tony's arm and made his way downstairs, briefcase dangling from one hand. His expression didn't give much away, but Charity could've sworn he looked relieved.

She grabbed her jacket and made her way downstairs and outside. Since the morning briefing had been cancelled, they hadn't exactly missed anything. Tony joined her and draped an arm over her shoulders.

"What's on your schedule today?" she asked him.

"Frank and I are due to meet with the new recruits in half an hour. You?" He smiled, but his eyes looked tired, and she understood how much effort he'd expended working on Milton, particularly when he'd sent cells from his own body across the divide to heal Milton's mind.

"I'm supposed to meet the women in the practice arena in forty-five minutes to work on our mind meld exercises." She paused a beat. "We have time. Do you want breakfast or at least coffee?"

"Both would be great. How about if you come to the lab? I want to talk, and the cafeteria's not very private."

"You keep food there?" She felt surprised.

"Of course." He rolled his eyes. "I get immersed in things. If I didn't have a ready source of calories, I'd have starved long since. Come on."

He moved his arm off her shoulders and clasped one of her hands as they made their way across the Langley campus. "That was awfully close," he said after a long silence.

"I figured. When you shoved energy into him to stop the seizures, it seemed like a last ditch effort."

"It was. I couldn't think of anything else to do. Frank counseled against it, but if we hadn't, Milton would've died, or turned into a vegetable. The brain can't tolerate back-to-back seizures for much longer than that."

"Any idea what a regular doctor would've done?" She ducked under his arm when he held the door into his lab building open.

"Pumped him full of drugs to stop the seizures. Unfortunately, he'd never have come back around. The vibrational instability would've escalated, even with him unconscious."

"Which way?" Charity looked up and down a long corridor dotted with doors.

"Up those stairs." Tony pointed and waited for her to start climbing before he followed.

Partway down the third floor hallway, he slapped his palm against a reader plate and opened the door to his lab. Charity had never been there, and she took a few moments to register rows of glass-fronted cabinets, bookshelves, two computer stations with huge screens, and generous worktables. "It's a nice workspace," she ventured.

"It is. Much better than what I had at the compound."

She squared her shoulders and turned to face him. "I want to say something."

He stiffened. "Aw, Christ! If you're going to tell me you're having second thoughts again—"

She laid a hand over his mouth. "Hush. Hear me out. I was really proud of you this morning. You work with a quiet competence that inspires others to believe in you. You're not hasty. You think things through. I felt the same way watching you while we were in that infernal swamp."

The tense planes of his face softened, and something warm and tender flickered in his eyes. "Thank you. I'm not used to compliments. In truth, I'm not sure I've ever had one directed at me before."

"You're welcome, but I'm not done. I had a chance to do some thinking back there in Milton's bedroom. What I came up with was this. I'm going to start assessing people as individuals, not as part of a group. You said something that hit home. I can't go back. I have to move forward."

Tony opened his mouth, changed his mind, and drew her against him. His heartbeat was solid and reassuring where she nestled her head in the crook of his neck. She threaded her arms around him, and he stroked her hair. "We all have to move forward," he murmured. "It's a different world than the one we were born into."

"Indeed it is. There's one more thing," she said. He waited, holding her, and she swallowed gallons of ambivalence and plowed forward. "Last night you told me you were falling in love with me. Well, I'm falling in love with you too. I wanted to make sure you knew."

He tightened his hold on her. "Charity, darling. Sweetheart, I— I'm just so goddamned grateful. You'll never be sorry. I give you my word. I'll take care of you. You'll never want for anything."

She lost herself in the touch of his body, wanting the moment to last forever, but reality intruded. "I'd love to stand here all day just like this, and listen to all the sweet nothings you can gin up, but you did promise me coffee and breakfast."

He kissed her forehead and let her go. "So I did." He trotted across the room. Once he got there, he rustled around and lit a Bunsen burner, placing a glass carafe over it.

Charity giggled. "Don't you have a microwave?"

"Sure, but this is almost as fast and much better for the environment—and for us." He rooted through a cabinet. "Cornflakes okay?"

"Do we have milk?"

"Of course. The chiller's behind you."

She located the stainless steel monstrosity, pulled a door open, and stifled a laugh. Sure enough, a milk carton was nestled in between what had to be tissue samples. She grasped it gingerly and carried it over to one of the long tables where Tony poured cereal into two bowls.

He grinned. "Nothing contagious in that chiller. I keep those samples in the locked one."

"Good to know." She smiled back, feeling light, buoyant, and full of an emotion she barely recognized.

Happy. I'm happy. So this is what it feels like.

Tony stirred hot water into instant coffee crystals and handed her a mug. Just as he sat down, the door to the lab burst open, and Faith and Hope strode into the room, pushing the door shut behind them.

"Something happened," Faith said without preamble.

"Yes." Hope seconded. "We want to know everything. Is there enough coffee to share? We already had breakfast."

Charity met Tony's gaze, and he shrugged. "May as well tell them," he said.

"May as well," Hope echoed. "We'll find out anyway. Coffee?"

"Help yourself," Tony said, "and pull up a stool."

"Hurry." Faith gestured with one hand. "We have to be at practice soon."

Tony burst out laughing. "Pushy. Tough. Bitchy. You're amazing. All of you."

"We think so too." Charity grinned at him and dug into her cornflakes.

CHAPTER 18

Charity loped across the practice area in the underground arena, intent on gathering fresh clothes from the women's changing room. They'd been honing their mental linkage with each other and the five new Nameless Ones for the past day and a half. Charlie, Milton, Roy, and Roy's team trained with them, while Frank and Tony were hot at work in the lab making isomeric changes in Cortexiphan that would cut down on side effects for humans.

Good thing.

Watching Milton's body spasm endlessly had been nerve-wracking. Charity felt helpless, torn between a desire to shield Honor and the need to do something, anything, to alleviate Milton's suffering.

Two weeks had passed since Milton's near-death experience, and he'd bounced back stronger than ever, and with psi abilities to rival her own. True to her prediction, the other men all wanted the same augmentation. She rolled her eyes and ducked into the locker room. For some unknown reason, no one looked too deeply into just why Milton had turned himself into a guinea pig for the drug, but the CIA dug its heels in about not allowing anyone else access to it until it was less toxic.

"Hey there!" Hope and Faith ran up behind her. Hope clapped her on the back. "How're you doing?"

"What do you mean how am I doing?" Charity scoffed at the question. "You've been working with me in that fucking arena since yesterday. You know exactly how I'm doing. I want out of here."

"She means, how's Tony?" Faith drew out his name and waggled her eyebrows at Charity.

Heat started in her chest and swooshed over her head. How was Tony, indeed? "Fine," she managed and turned away before the women could rib her about her cheek-to-cheek grin and reddened face.

"That's all we get?" Hope persisted.

"We want juicy details," Faith cut in. "You've been far more close-mouthed than Honor and Glory were about their men."

"Some things should stay private," Charity retorted and shucked her sweaty exercise pants, sports bra, and T-shirt.

"We've never had secrets," Hope protested.

"Speaking of which." Charity rounded on her and pulled a clean sweatshirt over her head, "How's Charlie?"

"How would I know? You've seen as much of him as I have."

Charity stepped into a pair of jeans and sat on a bench to get into her running shoes and socks. They trained barefoot to enhance their agility. When she looked up, Faith and Hope were mostly dressed too.

"Have you told him you like him?" she asked Hope.

The other woman blushed and shook her head. "Hell, no. I report to him." She snorted. "If we keep hooking up with the available men, the CIA will kick us out rather than perennially reassigning us to different team leaders."

"It's not that bad," Faith said. "You could partner up with that team that has the new Nameless Ones. David's heading it up."

"First, I'd have to have a reason to request a switch, and I don't. We haven't even shared a cup of coffee." Hope stuffed her arms into a jacket. "Ready to go?"

"More than ready," Charity said. "I appreciate that they feed us down here, but I miss daylight and being outside."

"Yeah, what you really miss is Tony," Hope said.

"That too," Charity agreed. "I'm looking forward to seeing him tonight. Maybe he and Frank have had luck shaping the Cortexiphan into a molecule that's easier for normal humans to tolerate."

Hope started for the door, but turned back. "We didn't have that drug before the rebellion, did we?"

"Yeah, humans had it before then," Charity said. "No one believed what it could do, and because it was dangerous, it got shelved. We were the only ones who truly wanted it. The human scientists were gun-shy."

"Probably worried someone would sue them." Faith left the locker room at a fast jog. Charity and Hope paced her.

They exited the building into a chill wind. A lovely sunset painted the western horizon in shades of teal, violet, and pink. Charity began to lope toward the building that held Tony's lab, but she stopped dead and stared at the colors in the sky for long moments, waving goodbye to the other women.

"Charity. Can you hear me?" Tony's voice made her smile.

"Yeah. I'm above ground. Got waylaid by the sunset. It's pretty spectacular."

"I know. I can see it out my windows." He paused a beat. *"I'd love to share it with you."*

"Be there in five."

She broke into a trot, still smiling. Things with Tony had been better than good. They'd been amazing, incredible. The longer they spent together, the easier it was to lose herself in the special world they created. The sex was hot and amazing, but Tony was so much more than a vehicle to satisfy her body. He fed her mind. And her soul. He was bright, funny, creative, and courageous. It had taken far more guts for him to leave the compound than for her to do the same thing. She'd been a second-class citizen with little to lose, whereas he lost everything.

The outer building door clicked open for her, and she knew he'd been tracking her energy across Langley's campus. Distance melted away as she took the stairs two at a time.

He met her at the top of the stairwell and drew her into a tight embrace, kissing her forehead and cheeks. "I've missed you, sweetheart."

Charity leaned into him, enjoying the feel of his body against hers. "Missed you too. Your apartment or mine tonight?"

"How about yours? But first, come into the lab."

"Did you and Frank figure out the Cortexiphan puzzle?"

He nodded, his eyes alight with enthusiasm. "At least the first stages. We're running one last test, and I want to check the results. Then we can go."

She walked beneath his arm when he held the laboratory door open for her. Frank glanced up and smiled. "Guess Tony told you about the potentially good news?"

"He did. You must be thrilled."

Frank nodded. "I am. I've been living in this lab ever since Milton's mishap." He snorted. "The research would've gone faster but he…" He jabbed an index finger Tony's way. "…insisted on spending his evenings with you. At least the ones when you weren't closeted in the underground arena."

"Can you blame me?" Tony grinned and made his way to a workbench teeming with slides and beakers.

"No. If I had a woman waiting for me, I wouldn't have been here, either."

Charity quirked a brow. Coming from Frank, that was downright chatty, since he'd never been much for personal disclosure.

A long, low whistle blasted from across the room, and Tony fist pumped the air. "Woot! We did it." He straightened from his lab stool, where he'd been hunched over a binocular scope.

"It would appear so," Frank said. "At least in a petri dish. Next thing we'll need to run are at least a few animal studies."

"Once we get the word out about this…" Charity spoke thoughtfully. "…maybe the Nameless Ones will think twice about attacking again."

Frank narrowed his eyes. "Maybe so. It's been damned quiet ever since that last go round. I figure they're cranking up for something major."

"Well, it's not going to happen tonight." Tony spun Charity around and gave her a gentle push toward the door. "We're out of here."

"Not that you asked, but I'll lock up," Frank called after them.

"Thanks," Tony shot back. "I owe you one."

"Hell, you owe me significantly more than that. Remember—"

The door shut, cutting off further words. "Do you have anything we could eat?" Tony asked.

Charity nodded. "Nothing fancy, but we still have frozen pizza and salad stuff."

"Perfect." He threaded an arm around her waist and snugged her against him, nuzzling her neck. "Wonder if they'd mind if I just moved in with you?"

She laughed. "If by *they* you mean the CIA, I have no idea. Were you planning to ask me what I thought of the idea?"

"Okay." He set a gentle pace toward her apartment. "What do you think of it?"

Charity turned it over. They spent all their time together anyway, so it made sense, but that was on an intellectual level. She dug deep and accessed her feelings. Did she want to share everything with the man by her side?

When the answer came, it was so obvious her heart took flight in a flood of warm, fluttery delight. "Yes," she said.

"Yes, what?" he prodded.

"Yes, I'm all for it. Wonder if they have quarters designated for couples?"

"Not sure, let me check the map of this place that I downloaded." He was silent for a long moment and then shook his head. "Can't find what I was looking for, so I'm not sure, but we can ask Milton."

"Good plan." They'd made it to her building, and she tipped her chin to activate the retinal scanner to let them inside. "If anyone can find us a place to live, he can."

"No kidding." Tony chuckled. "He's been like a different man, not nearly so stand-offish ever since—"

"Ssht," Charity cautioned as they walked past the guard. She smiled pleasantly, and he nodded in their direction.

"Guess I've been chattier too." Tony grinned and stood aside for her to enter the stairwell first.

"Not just chattier. I don't think I'd ever truly seen you smile before." She topped the stairs. Excited to be alone with her man, she half jogged to her door and pushed it open with her mind.

"I didn't have much to smile about before you." Tony followed her inside, kicking the door shut behind them.

Charity unlaced her shoes and toed them off. She turned to face him and held out her arms. He swept her into a tight embrace, holding her against him for long moments as he ran his hands up and down her back. His cock swelled against her belly, and heat threaded between her thighs. No matter how many times they made love, it didn't dull her desire for more of him.

"Looks like another midnight supper," she said.

"I could say something like 'you're all the food I need', but it sounds sappy, even to me."

"That's okay." She moved back far enough to unzip his jacket and slide it over his shoulders. "I don't remember anyone cooing over me—ever. I'll take all the sappy I can get."

He let go of her long enough to pull his top over his head and remove her jacket and sweatshirt. A muted gasp blew past his lips, and he reached for her bare breasts. "I've seen you lots of times, but every single time, the view gets better. You've got the most amazing breasts." He made a low, decidedly masculine sound and filled his hands with them, rubbing his thumbs over her nipples until they were achingly hard.

Breath hitched in her throat, suddenly thick with wanting him, and she stroked fingertips over his copper-colored nipples until they were tight buds of lust. The tented front of his trousers drew her like a Siren's song, and she grappled with his belt, button, and zipper.

He caught his pants before they could pool at his feet and sat on the edge of the couch to unlace his boots and tug them off. His gaze never left her body. Something wild and untamed flared in the depths of his eyes. She adored that look, the one that turned him dangerous and fierce, and so desirable it took every shred of self-control not to throw herself on top of him.

He saved her the trouble. "Come here." His voice was harsh with need, and he placed his hands on either side of her waist and pulled her onto his lap, so she straddled him, kneeling on the couch. He undid her pants and moved her enough to slide them down her legs, followed by her panties, before resettling her so she faced him.

His erection pushed directly on her clit, and she writhed against him, awash in sensation pulsing through her. He swung his hands to her butt, holding on, and thrust against her, his cock jamming into her nubbin with each shove. Angling his head, he caught a nipple in his mouth and sucked hard, just the way she liked it.

She threaded her fingers beneath his hair and held on, knowing orgasm was imminent. He loved to bring her off, to watch her come. He'd told her that often. Sure enough, he let go of her nipple and moved a hand between her legs where he increased the pressure on her clit. Climax ripped out of her, and she pushed hard against his fingers and his cock, wringing every last flicker of pleasure from it.

His pants were already undone, so she reached inside and drew his cock out, stroking it with eager fingers. He was perfect, so hot and hard and long that when she wasn't fucking him, she imagined it and had dreams where he took her from every conceivable angle, leaving her shaken and gasping, just like she was now.

Charity wriggled down until she knelt between his legs and licked the tip of his cock, tasting the salt of semen already oozing out. She'd learned what he liked too, and she stroked him with hands and tongue. He groaned and thrust into her mouth, giving himself over to pleasure.

They usually started with giving each other at least one climax before they got down to serious fucking. Charity tightened her grip on his ridged flesh, loving how he filled her mouth and the hot, hungry sounds he made.

He pulled out of her mouth, surprising her. She wasn't done, but then neither was he. "What?" She gazed up at him.

"Something different." He grinned, looking boyish and beautiful, his coppery skin glowing with desire and his eyes alight. He slid to the floor next to her. "I want you to watch me come, and I want to watch you touch yourself."

Her belly clenched with need. She'd always wanted to watch semen spurt from him, but he'd been inside her body every time. He slipped inside her mind. Charity adored the dual feedback loop, where she experienced his arousal as sharply as she felt her own. Traveling the link to his body, she sensed his balls tight against his body, felt the tension in his cock. Beyond that, she was aware of lust and protectiveness, all aimed at her.

He leaned back against the couch, legs splayed on the floor. She threw a leg over each of his facing him, and closed her mouth over his. He cradled her head between his hands and dove into the kiss, playing with her tongue and lips, withdrawing, and coming back for more. Somewhere in the midst of that kiss, her fingers found her clit and began to rub.

He drew back and closed a hand over his erection, his gaze hot and intense focused on her body. He stroked himself, moving hard and fast. Through their mind link, she felt his arousal expand until it filled all her senses, felt his seed, burning and urgent, boil from balls to cock, and watched as it spurted out in thick flashes of white heat.

Her climax caught her by surprise, sweeping through her so powerfully, it blasted from her toes to the tip of her head. A shriek burst from her throat so primitive, she scarcely recognized her own voice, and then Tony closed his arms around her and pulled her tight against his chest.

Still in her mind, he murmured, *"That was perfect. Amazing. God, I love you."* There was more, but he faded to incoherence.

She nestled her head in the curve of his shoulder. "Do you suppose it will always be like this? Where we can't get enough of each other."

"I don't see why not."

A laugh bubbled from her belly. "I can think of lots of reasons."

He moved so he could gaze into her face. "I could excise that part of your brain. Or I could just make certain you're always as happy as you are right now."

A tender smile curved the corners of her mouth. "That cuts both ways. I want to take care of you too."

"Then we shouldn't have any problems." His eyes glittered mischievously. "What do you want next? Dinner or more loving?"

"They're not mutually exclusive. Food will give us more staying power."

"A woman after my own heart. Why don't you shower? By the time you're done, I'll have our supper laid out."

"You don't have to ask twice." She winked and cupped the side of his face. "One of my dirty little secrets is I can't cook."

"I figured that out, but I love you anyway."

"I really like hearing that. No one's ever loved me before." She teased the perfect bones of his face with her fingertips.

"We're even," he said. "No one's ever loved me, either."

Sandwiched between them, his cock, which hadn't subsided much, began to swell again. "Better get moving, wench..." He brushed his lips over hers, and helped her to her feet. "...before I change my mind."

Charity shrugged. "Food now. Food later. That's not what's important. You're important. You and me, and the joy we bring each other."

Tony got to his feet. A smile flickered in the depths of his eyes. She soaked in the tenderness in that look, filled with all his hopes and dreams for the two of them, and it took her breath away. She tried for words, but gave up.

"I love you too," she said and watched the expression in his eyes deepen, overflowing with a feral protectiveness that thrilled her to her bones.

"Are you going to keep an eye on me while I make dinner?" He quirked a roguish brow.

"I could die a happy woman watching you do damn near anything."

"That was the right answer. If you want a shower, now's a good time."

"I can take a hint." Charity turned away and floated into the bathroom, so happy she thought she might shatter into a million motes of light. Tomorrow was soon enough to focus on the ongoing war with her kind, training the new recruits, and Cortexiphan. Tonight, it was just her and Tony, and that reality filled her with delight and confidence in their future.

For someone who was convinced I'd spend my life alone, I've travelled a long road.

Laughter bubbled as she flipped on the taps and stepped over the rim of the tub into water streaming from the fancy massage showerhead Tony bought her as a gift. It wasn't easy to accept things from him—or anyone else—but she was working on that. For the first time ever she had things to look forward to, and she planned to savor every single one of them.

YOU'VE REACHED the end of *Claiming Charity*. Read on for a sample of *Loving Hope*.

ABOUT THE AUTHOR

Ann Gimpel is a USA Today bestselling author. A lifelong aficionado of the unusual, she began writing speculative fiction a few years ago. Since then her short fiction has appeared in a number of webzines, magazines, and anthologies. Her longer books run the gamut from urban fantasy to paranormal romance to science fiction. Once upon a time, she nurtured clients. Now she nurtures dark, gritty fantasy stories that push hard against reality. When she's not writing, she's in the backcountry getting down and dirty with her camera. She's published over 50 books to date, with several more planned for 2018 and beyond. A husband, grown children, grandchildren, and wolf hybrids round out her family.

Keep up with her at www.anngimpel.com or http://anngimpel.blogspot.com

If you enjoyed what you read, get in line for special offers and pre-release special reads. Sign up for Ann's newsletter on her website or her blog.

GENTECH REBELLION, BOOK FOUR

*H*ope blinked dirt out of her eyes and stifled a groan. She didn't want to risk an energy flare looking for the others. Doing anything other than keeping her resources muffled was an enormous risk.

She took a mouthful of water from the canteen hanging off her field belt and swished it around her mouth. Time had passed since a blast hit her helicopter, knocking it out of the air. Maybe as much as an hour. Things happened fast after the bird was hit, and her team leader, Charlie McClaren, folded her hand around the ripcord on her parachute.

He'd all but pushed her out the open chopper door with exhortations to, "Watch out for the rotor, goddammit."

A few other choice instructions were lost in the slipstream as she plummeted from the dying aircraft, her pounding heart stenciling fear from her head to her toes.

What was supposed to be a simple out-and-back mission had turned into something much more complex, never mind much more dangerous. She'd been expecting Charlie or Frank to materialize ever since she cut herself out of the tree her chute got tangled in, but neither man showed up.

She didn't understand why. They couldn't have landed very far away after the crash—assuming they made it out of the chopper intact. Too rattled by her first actual parachute jump, she'd neglected to watch for the other chutes, which would've told her the location of her teammates.

Were they dead? Or tripped up by the old growth forest?

She'd been careful chopping her way out of a particularly tall tree. Her caution ate up well over half an hour while she freed herself from where she swung thirty feet above the ground. She picked splinters out of her hands as she considered what to do next.

According to the GPS in her augmented brain, she was in a wooded corridor in north Central Maine. She, Charlie, and Frank had been on a routine mission to pick up Cortexiphan, an experimental drug banned by the FDA, from a freak compound near Bangor. Not that they'd expected the freaks—a renegade group of genetically modified humans who wanted to take down the U.S. government—to just hand over the drug, but military planes had annihilated the settlement. No one expected it would be difficult to waltz in and locate the chemical.

Hope shook her head. Underestimating her people was always a mistake. The genetically modified were smarter, stronger, faster, and more capable of pivoting in response to adverse conditions than normal humans ever dreamed of being.

She sheltered in a thick grove of some sort of deciduous tree and leaned against one of them. Could she risk her communicator? Would telepathy be safer? Hope grimaced. Freaks had to be behind the attack on her chopper, which meant nothing was safe. Who else would shoot down a CIA chopper over U.S. soil?

She bit hard on her lower lip. She understood freaks—how they thought, what made them tick—because she was one. She'd escaped the compounds, though, and left that life behind.

"What do I do now?"

She started at the sound of her voice, not realizing she'd spoken aloud until she heard the words. A quick glance at the sky told her she didn't have much daylight left to work with. Not that it mattered. She could always dial in her night vision, but it held a particular energy signature.

The flash of warmth in Charlie's hazel eyes as he'd covered her hand with his, instructing her how to yank the ripcord, filled her mind. She liked him. A lot. But he barely knew she existed beyond working under him. She'd made a few pathetic attempts at flirting, but he'd ignored her. Maybe her shy smiles were so subtle, he hadn't interpreted them the way she hoped, but that probably wasn't it. She was a freak. He was a normal human, and a goddamned good-looking one at that. He could have his pick of women. No reason on earth to look twice at her.

Much like the genetically altered men she'd spent her life with, Charlie was tall and rangy, with dark hair and hazel eyes. He was addicted to danger the same as all CIA operatives. When twin fires burned in the backs of his eyes, it was all she could do not to throw herself into his arms and beg him to take her.

Here.

Now.

In front of everyone.

She tossed her head, muffling a snort. She knew next to nothing about men, sex, or love. Her entire primer on all things human was derived from hours of television and the Internet. Her other source of information came from pumping Honor, Glory, and Charity, three of her closest friends, about their relationships with CIA agents they'd hooked up with.

A branch crackled behind her. Hope lunged for her sidearm, thought better of it, and focused her mental kinetics. She didn't loose anything—not yet. Power ran through her in high voltage jolts. Holding it in abeyance wasn't easy, but she needed to know what she faced. The minute she targeted someone, her ability would glow like a beacon, alerting any genetically modified human in the area to both her presence and precise location.

"Hope! I've been hunting for you ever since the chopper crashed."

Frank limped from behind a bush. He was well over six feet tall with heavy slabs of muscle providing superior physical abilities. Genetically modified like her, his shaggy dark hair brushed his shoulders, and his amber animal-like eyes with vertical slit pupils came close to radiating joy. Given Frank's taciturn ways, that said a lot.

She siphoned off the lethal force dancing through her body an electron at a time. "Fuck!" She trotted to his side. "I almost killed you."

A crooked grin lent him a boyish appearance. "I felt the energy build. Figured I needed to say something."

Hope took a closer look. A wicked looking gash ran from below Frank's right eye to his cheekbone, and his hands were abraded and bleeding. She ran a hand down his body, scanning for injuries.

Before she was done, he batted it away. "I twisted my ankle when I landed in a bramble thicket. It's how I got so banged up—fighting my way out of thorns as long as my thumb. I've instituted a healing program. Should be better than new in a few hours." Breath hissed from between his teeth. "Shit! After my last impromptu exit from a chopper, I promised myself I'd practice parachuting, but somehow I never freed up the time."

"Yeah well, I've never even come close to doing anything like jumping out of a helicopter. Didn't like it much. Any idea where Charlie is?"

Frank shook his head. "I was hoping he'd be with you."

"We may not have had all that fancy commando training, but I never would've guessed how easy it is to lose someone between an auto-rotating helicopter and the ground."

"We have to locate him." Frank narrowed his eyes, or he might have winced, she couldn't tell. "You haven't expended any power, or I'd have found you sooner. Charlie certainly hasn't used any."

"It's not safe. Charlie must've figured that out." She crossed her arms under her breasts. "Freaks did this, huh?"

He cocked his head to one side. "Who else? I'm surprised you asked. Their signature is all over it."

Hope shrugged, feeling uncomfortable for missing something obvious. "Maybe it is. Once the chopper started going nuts, I kind of stopped thinking."

He looked at her then. Really looked and ran his own scan of her systems before she could move out of range.

"I'm all right." She took a few steps away. "If I wasn't, I'd have told you."

"Needed to check for myself," he said gruffly. "We have more latitude with two of us—but only if we're able to tap into all of our abilities."

"What's that supposed to mean?" She frowned, still not feeling a hundred percent.

His face settled into the patronizing lines she associated with Nameless Ones, genetically modified men who'd made her life hell when they lived in compounds. All of them—men and women alike—were products of genetic research originally hatched up by the U.S. government. Appalled by how they were treated, they staged a rebellion, and blew up the breeding farms. While women had been an integral part of the rebellion, they'd been relegated to second-class citizenry after a few years of living in hidden compounds. Their abilities were superior to the men's, and the men had been frightened of losing the upper hand—

"It means we need to risk exposure to find Charlie. We can't leave without him." Frank's words broke into her thoughts, and she shelved her foray into the past.

Hope set her jaw in determination and moved back to Frank's side, so she could join her mental energy with his more easily. "Ready."

"Before we do something that's certain to compromise us, have you looked for him?"

"Not really. My chute got stuck in a tree, and it took a ridiculous amount of time to free myself. I was just getting my bearings and deciding what to do next when you showed up."

Frank made a chopping motion with one hand. "Enough. I don't need the long version."

The same anger she always felt when a Nameless One got heavy handed flared hot and bright. "You don't run things anymore. Stop ordering me around." She curled one hand into a fist and punched the air in his direction.

"I wasn't—" His nostrils flared with annoyance, but he bit off the rest of his sentence. "Never mind. You're already in my head. We'll do a short, fast scan. Thirty seconds tops."

A frisson of apprehension ran down her spine. What if Charlie were dead?

He can't be. He just can't.

Why not? Men in his line of work die all the time...

"Hope!" Frank's voice cut like a bullwhip. "I don't give a fuck how you feel about him. Help me do this."

Heat blotched her chest and face. "Sorry," she mumbled. "Told you before that I was ready, and I still am."

"On my count. One. Two. Three."

Hope shot energy in tandem with Frank's. Relief filled her when Charlie's unique energy indicator pinged back clean and pure. "Yes!" She pumped the air with her already fisted hand.

Frank shot an odd glance her way. "He's alive," he said slowly.

The same clammy uneasiness she'd felt before they looked settled across her shoulders like a yoke, and she made a come along gesture with two fingers. "Whatever it is. Spill it."

"He's in a compound."

"What?" Hope wasn't sure she'd heard right. "Didn't we bomb the fuck out of the one up here?"

"One of them, yeah." Frank drew his brows into a thick, worried line. "There's another about a mile from our current position. Apparently that one's still online and functional."

She reached for her wrist computer, intent on radioing Langley to send reinforcements, but Frank shook his head. "Why not?" She chewed her lower lip. "We can't take on a whole compound by ourselves."

"If we radio for help, they'll hear. If they're on the fence about killing Charlie, it could send them over the edge and sign his death warrant."

She unclenched her fist and flexed her fingers, forcing order out of the chaos her mind had become. "Langley will know something's wrong. They'll have tracked our craft with radar."

"Yes, and they'll know we're no longer in the air. Them sending assistance without us asking for it isn't a problem."

"Tell me what you're thinking." She batted back a frantic need to storm the freaks' fortress and kill the men one by one. Anything to get Charlie out of their clutches alive.

Frank shifted to closely shielded telepathic speech. *"It's a long shot, but what I think might work is..."*

CHARLIE MANHANDLED Hope to get her outside the chopper. He recognized the wild look in her eyes and kicked himself roundly for not prioritizing exit training for all the women on his team. Frank was another story. He'd adopted a stoic expression and stepped past Charlie into open air.

Intuition on overdrive, Charlie followed his people, tapping a coded distress message through his wrist computer after he deployed his chute. HQ might not pick it up right away, but it wasn't the end of the world. He liked it when the other side turned up the heat. It kept things interesting. Besides, the CIA would figure out their bird wasn't airborne soon enough. In the meantime, maybe he could find a freak or two to grill for data.

Veteran of hundreds of jumps, Charlie twisted sideways and slipped handily through the forest canopy. He rolled to the ground, gathering his chute almost before he had his feet under him. Folding and stuffing on autopilot, he figured he'd survey his surroundings then locate Frank and Hope.

Hope.

Warmth flared at the thought of her. Hell, more than warmth. The woman was hotter than a boatload of Sirens with her long, dark hair and cat-green eyes. Tall, like all the genetically modified woman, her shapely form mixed muscle with curves in the right places. His body came alive as he pictured her, but he told it to stand down. No matter how sensual Hope was, it didn't matter. He was done with females. They only got in the way. He'd never had a relationship where they didn't start trying to change him as soon as he took them to bed. It was subtle at first but became more strident when he ignored their cues. He'd been married once. Never again.

His bachelor status and Black Ops lifestyle played hell with his sex life, but the freedom was worth it.

He shouldered his pack with the chute folded inside and sent a short blast of energy outward, surveying his surroundings. He'd taken a series of injections to make himself more like the freaks. While using his augmented power wasn't exactly second nature, he'd gotten more comfortable with it over time.

His power slapped back at him so hard his ears rang, and he did a double take. That had never happened before. What the fuck?

Slowly, more cautious this time, he paid out energy, seeking the characteristic pings that belonged to humans versus freaks versus animal life. Answers bombarded him, and adrenaline poured through his system. He raised his AK-47 to his shoulder and scanned the thick tree cover for the enemy.

His finger flirted with the trigger. Were Hope and Frank close enough to wound or kill with a stray bullet? He hadn't sensed them. What nearly mowed him down was the realization he was surrounded by at least twenty freaks. Maybe twenty-five.

Fuck! Crap! Goddammit!

He tightened his fingers around the gun. If he didn't mount

offensive action damned fast, the freaks would take him out. He pushed his power wide open, seeking his people. An odd sensation hit him right between the eyes. He fought it, but the rifle dropped from his hands, and his knees buckled. His back bowed painfully just before darkness hit him like a sledgehammer.

~

POUNDING temples brought Charlie jolting back to consciousness. His head hurt like a bitch. He wanted to rub it and jerked a hand upward only to have it stop. A cuff tightened painfully around his wrist, and he lowered his arm.

He forced his eyes open and twisted his head from side to side. It made the pain worse, but he had to know if he had anything to work with. He lay on his back on a thin pallet spread over a concrete floor. His wrists were cuffed to bolts set in the concrete, but his ankles were free. The room was rectangular and small. Light filtered in through a window covered with a torn shade. Beyond his pallet, the space was empty. A stout wooden door was set into the far wall. Metal staves crisscrossed along its length.

Charlie scooted his butt back and adopted a bent over seated position. Freaks had shot down his chopper. It had to be retribution for the CIA knocking out several of their compounds. Regardless of their motives, they'd set a net and captured him. He made a sideways chopping motion to free one hand, but got nowhere. He hadn't expected it to work, but being helpless wasn't his style.

Christ!

Were Frank and Hope somewhere in this building right along with him? He pushed his mind voice outward, but it exploded in his head. Spots danced in front of his eyes, and he bit back a muffled yelp of pain. It felt as if someone were slicing through his head right behind his eyes with a buzz saw.

He took shallow breaths until he had the upper hand again. He'd be goddamned if he'd turn into a whimpering ninny because of a little discomfort. He took stock of his situation. No telepathy; that was abundantly clear. No wrist computer. Naturally, they'd taken it. Also no rifle, no sidearm, no knives, no communicator, no sat phone.

Focus! There's always a way. I have to find it.

What could he do? He'd been in almost the same situation in the Middle East—not dealing with genetically altered men, but with Al Qaida, who were almost as bad in some respects, and much worse in others. They wrote the book where *ruthless* was concerned. The freaks were pikers by comparison.

Charlie forced himself to breathe. To think. He had an opportunity since they'd left him alone, clearly convinced he was toast. He was an engineer by trade. He'd majored in aeronautical engineering before he joined the Navy Seals and put in three tours in the Middle East. It was where he met Milton, who convinced him to sign on with the CIA. That had been a few years ago, and he'd never looked back.

He focused on the cuffs, recognizing them as an older style that gave way to determined probing. He pawed through the pockets he could reach, seeking something as simple as a paperclip, but without success. Pain throbbed from his lower lip. He'd bitten so hard on it, he'd drawn blood.

Licking away the salty substance, an idea took shape. He couldn't use his power to project anything beyond the ten by twelve foot room he'd been tossed into, but maybe he could marshal it on a local basis.

He focused a thin thread of kinetics at one of the cuffs, ready to draw back the second it boomeranged on him, but it never happened. The cuff warmed, and then became uncomfortably hot. Smoke rose, and the stench of his own flesh burning filled his nostrils.

"Come on, you motherfucker," he growled. "Open."

Maybe it was the words, but his right cuff popped its catch. Charlie didn't waste time savoring his victory. He repeated his actions on the left cuff and sprang to his feet the moment it loosened. He eyed the door, but discarded it immediately. If the freaks had posted a guard, he'd be in the corridor.

Silent as a panther, he sidled to the side of the window and twitched the shade aside. His eyes widened. The goddamned window had a latch. How could the freaks have been so stupid?

Because they never thought I could free myself.

Maybe they don't know I had the injections to make me more like them.

Charlie worked as efficiently as he could. Fast and quiet would get him out of here. A glance told him he was in a ground level room. Piece of cake. He jimmied the sash and waited, barely breathing.

Nothing.

No patrols, no foot traffic outside what had to be a compound. He recalled the master map of the compound locations, but reeled himself in before that exercise went very far. He had no idea where he was. He could've been out for hours, and they might've moved him a long way from where they'd shot his bird out of the sky.

Didn't matter.

He let himself out the window and crouched on the ground, scanning everything he could see. Once he was convinced he had a clear shot, he made for the surrounding woods. Time enough to sort things out from there.

The important thing was he was free. This was the USA, not the hinterlands of Iraq or Afghanistan. All he had to do was find a dwelling and put in a call to Langley. Even if Frank and Hope were being held prisoner, there wasn't much he could do as a solo operative to free them without weapons or ammunition.

No. His best bet—and their best chance for survival—was calling in reinforcements as fast as he could. Ignoring what felt like knives cutting through his temples from the headache that hadn't abated much, he slid from tree to tree until he'd put half a mile between him and the compound. By then his head felt a little better, and he broke into jog, navigating via the augmented programming in his mind. He wasn't as competent as a full-blooded freak, but he was better than before the injections.

Much better.

A straight line heading west should bring him to farms that dotted this part of Maine, and sooner rather than later. Charlie put his head down and ran for all he was worth. His team needed him, and he'd do his damnedest to ensure their survival.